What readers are saying...

Stephanie C., age 14
It is very hard for me to have faith in God sometimes, but Millie's courage has helped me get through my bad times and turn them into good ones. She is definitely a role model for all girls, whether they be 4, 14, or 40! I can't wait to read the next book!

Lindsey K., age 13
I bought the new Millie books. They are just wonderful! I couldn't put them down from the moment I got them. In fact, I started reading them in the car on the way home from the store! It's my dream to become like Millie, and of course, Jesus. Millie is a great character. She is so easy to relate to. It really feels like she's a friend from another time!!

Melissa A., age 12
I really LOVE the Millie books! I seriously think they are the best I've ever read. I'm like Millie when it comes to walking with God. The Bible verses in the book helped me a lot, and I also realized I need to spend more time with God.

Hayley L., age 11
The Millie books are superb! Not only are they exciting, and thrilling, but they are great books to help girls grow in their relationship with God! I also like the Millie books because I can relate to alot of her problems. I strongly encourage YOU, if you haven't already, to read the Millie series! I guarantee that YOU WILL LOVE THEM!!! I can't be separated from them!

Katherine L., age 10
I LOVE the Millie stories. They are the best books I have ever read. I have seven brothers and sisters and when I realized how patient she was, I wanted to be just like her. I love her faith in God. It had a great affect on my life.

Millie's Unsettled Season

BOOK ONE
of the
A Life of Faith:
Millie Keith
Series

Based on the beloved books by
Martha Finley

MCP
Mission City Press

Franklin, Tennessee

Book One of the *A Life of Faith: Millie Keith* Series

Millie's Unsettled Season
Copyright © 2001, Mission City Press, Inc. All Rights Reserved.

Published by Mission City Press, Inc.

This book is based on the *Mildred Keith* novels written by Martha Finley and first published in 1876 by Dodd, Mead & Company.

Adaptation Written by:	Kersten Hamilton
Cover & Interior Design:	Richmond & Williams
Cover Photography:	Michelle Grisco Photography
Typesetting:	BookSetters
Special Thanks to:	Cindy Sterling

For more information, write to Mission City Press at 202 Second Avenue South, Franklin, Tennessee 37064, or visit our Web Site at:

www.alifeoffaith.com

Library of Congress Catalog Card Number: 2001117167
Finley, Martha
     Millie's Unsettled Season
     Book One of the *A Life of Faith: Millie Keith* Series
     ISBN: 1-928749-09-7

Printed in the United States of America
5 6 7 8 — 07 06 05

DEDICATION

This book is
dedicated to
the memory of
MARTHA FINLEY

*Martha Finley was a woman of God
clearly committed to advancing the cause of Christ
through stories of people who sought
to reflect Christian character in everyday life.
Although written in an era very different from ours,
her works still inspire both young and old
to seek to know and follow the living God.*

— FOREWORD —

*I*n this book, the first of the *A Life of Faith: Millie Keith* Series, you are about to take a journey into the past. Your trip will begin in 1833, in the midwestern United States of America. As you will see, many things were different back then, but one central fact remains unchanged—the importance of family.

Our story begins in Lansdale, Ohio, a thriving town of its day. Lansdale is home to the Keiths—a large and happy family—and their oldest daughter, Millie. Millie is a bright twelve-year-old girl who is full of energy and good intentions. As the eldest child of eight boisterous brothers and sisters, Millie tries to be a big help to her loving, Christian parents. Together the family will travel west to start a new life in a young and undeveloped prairie town called Pleasant Plains, Indiana. There Millie will live among people, cultures, and traditions very foreign to her early childhood days and she will learn many lessons about living a life of faith.

The stories of Millie Keith, known formerly as the *Mildred Keith* novels, were published in 1876, eight years after the well-known *Elsie Dinsmore* books were introduced. Martha Finley, the creator of both characters, was a fascinating woman whose own life was the basis for part of the story of Millie Keith. Miss Finley was born in Ohio and moved to the Indiana Territory as a young girl—just like Millie.

This book is a careful adaptation of the original Mildred Keith story. In rewriting the books for modern readers, the

Christian message has been strengthened, the plot enhanced, and a number of new features have been added. Also included is a section on the history and social customs of the time period and a helpful family tree.

Millie's story is a portrait of courage and conviction, love of family and country, and a strong determination to live a life worthy of the Christian calling. We are confident that you will not only love Millie, but also find in her a model of the timeless virtues of Christian living.

Mission City Press is very proud to carry on Miss Finley's commitment to Biblical values by re-introducing Millie Keith to a new generation of readers. It is our sincere hope that you will gain many insights into your own life of faith as you follow Millie's exciting adventures.

∾ WELCOME TO MILLIE'S WORLD ∾

The westward expansion of the United States in the nineteenth century is one of the most thrilling chapters in our American history. Settlers who ventured out to find a better life in undeveloped territories faced challenges and hardships we can hardly imagine today. Obstacles, distresses, suffering, and miserable conditions met them constantly. It took great courage and vision to leave the comforts of home with established ways of living to plot uncharted paths to lands unknown.

During this time of the early 1800s, our young nation experienced the most rapid migration it would ever see, with Americans settling in large numbers in what is now called the Old Northwest Territory. The Northwest Ordinance of 1787 had provided for the governance of public lands there, establishing the process by which U.S. territories would

qualify for statehood. The Constitution of the United States went into effect in 1789 and gave Congress the power to regulate these territories, as the first lands surveyed under the Land Ordinance Act of 1785 were made available for sale. The settlements west of the Appalachian Mountains and east of the Mississippi River at the beginning of the 1800s were made by pioneers who felt the lure of the Northwest Territory, with its thick oak forests, rich farmland, rivers that made transporting goods and families possible, and land that was cheap—$1.25 for about half a hectare.

The Land Ordinance Act surveys changed the way towns, cities, and states were formed. To mark off property boundaries, people had previously used waterways, ridge tops, or tree lines, but over time trees died and streams dried up or shifted off course, making boundary lines difficult to determine. Recognizing that clear land titles were essential to the stability of our fast developing country, Congress ordered that a rectangular survey of all land be performed before it could be sold. Today, it is a source of amazement to fly over the vast lands west of the Appalachians and see the straight roads and rectangular fields that remain as a result of the Land Ordinance surveys.

In 1833, when our story begins, there were only twenty-four states in the United States. Ohio, where Millie lives at the outset of our story, became a state in 1803. Indiana, where the Keiths will be heading, was the nineteenth state admitted to the Union, achieving statehood in 1816. More than half the states that make up the United States today had not become states at this time. Andrew Jackson was sworn in on March 4, 1833, for his second term in office as the seventh President of the United States.

Millie's Unsettled Season

The day-to-day world in 1833 was very different from ours in many ways. For instance, without modern communication—radio, television, telephones, and the Internet—Millie and her family had to rely on letters to send and receive messages across town or across country. The mail, which was primarily delivered by stagecoach, was not reliable or quick in those days because scheduled stage routes in the unsettled territories and the Pony Express mail delivery would not start for almost thirty more years. A handwritten letter was a highly prized possession and would be read again and again as a treasure. People thought carefully about what they would say and how they would say it. An envelope could contain pages of local and family news accompanied by deeply felt prayers and Scripture references—all included for the reader's benefit and comfort.

Travel and transportation in Millie's time were also very different from today. Journeys of any great distance could take weeks and months. They were normally difficult and uncomfortable, and often unsafe. Walking was by far the primary means of transportation for short distances, but you will also read about travel on horses, carriages, stagecoaches, and wagons over long distances.

Riding on a stagecoach was not as romantic as old Western movies portray it to be. It was not smooth travel in roomy comfort. As many as eighteen to twenty passengers could be crammed together with mailbags and passenger luggage, with everything getting jostled by every bump, choked with dust, and all at the mercy of the natural elements. Before way stations (buildings set up every twenty miles or so that housed both stables and an eating room for stage passengers) were created in the 1860s, stagecoaches went for long distances without stopping. If

Foreword

the stage suffered a breakdown, passengers and cargo had to be unloaded while repairs were made. If the driver decided too much weight was to blame, mailbags were the first things to be overthrown — left abandoned by the wayside, never to reach their destination.

There were no national freeways like the ones we enjoy today. Pioneer Indiana was served by only two roads, and a large network of wagon paths. The federal government financed the building of the National Road that ran from Maryland to Illinois, with the Indiana portion (now U.S. Highway 40) completed in 1834. This horizontal road ran east to west through the center of the state, and the north-south Michigan Road ran from Madison, Indiana, in the south (on the Ohio River), straight up through Indianapolis to South Bend (on the St. Joseph River) near the northern state line. Thus Indiana became known as the "Crossroads of America" in the early 1800s.

Water travel was fast becoming the link from one place to another, with steamers, keelboats, packet boats, and sloops providing different forms of navigation. Man-made canals linked key rivers such as the Ohio to the Great Lakes, making commerce possible for inland states. The Ohio and Erie Canal, built between 1825 and 1832, brought prosperity to Ohio by making it possible for the farmers to market their goods in Cleveland, Chicago, and other larger cities. Packet boats were pulled up and down the canals by teams of mules or horses that walked along towpaths. Although they were slow, they were one of the safest ways to travel. Steamers had only been on the scene since around 1819, and journeys on them were still quite dangerous. Rivers were unpredictable at best, and high water periods brought even more dangers — uprooted trees

and floating logs could drive a boat off course. Steamer wrecks were not uncommon, and anyone journeying on one had to face the risks.

Keelboats were graceful, bow-bottomed freighters that used three means of locomotion to ensure passengers and cargo reached their destinations. About seventy feet long and eighteen feet wide, they contained a roofed cabin in the center, with a narrow walkway on each side, where six to twelve oarsmen would use bowed oars or long, straight poles to push the boat through the water. In addition, they contained a mast with a sail, and a "cordelle" (a long rope attached to the mast crossbar) for dragging the keelboat when water obstructions or weather conditions made it impossible to row, pole, or sail. Sloops were smaller and used for milder waters (like lakes) and shorter distances (frequent ports).

Providing for schools was a challenge for Indiana pioneer communities. The state constitution of 1816 directed the government to establish and maintain tax-supported schools free of charge, but the few tax dollars collected were spent for building roads and draining marshlands. School in the undeveloped land was, at best, held in a local one-room building, often times built by farming families who pitched in to help. More fortunate children were given the choice of attending the local school or learning at home under the guidance of their parents and other adults. Much like today, families who schooled their children at home would set up special rooms in which to teach, and multiple-aged children would all be taught together. This type of homeschooling required even more creativity than it does today, however, for there were no printed curriculum materials available, and the success of the education often depended upon the knowledge of the person teaching.

Foreword

The changing face of a free and growing society mirrored the growing pains that Millie felt as an adolescent girl. Unlike the Southern states, slavery had never been a common practice in the Northwest Territory, and was not tolerated in the unsettled prairie towns of Millie's world. These courageous men and women worked their land and built their towns and settlements without the aid of slaves. They were not, however, immune to their own prejudices. Exaggerated tales of savage Indian tribes spread like wildfire, causing the Native Americans to be disdained and feared by these settlers. Prior Indian wars provided some justification for their fears. For example, in the Black Hawk War of 1832, the last Indian war in the Northwest Territory, Chief Black Hawk and five hundred warriors, along with their families, came back across the Mississippi to take back their lands in Illinois. They were defeated in Wisconsin, and Black Hawk was returned to his people in Iowa after a year in prison.

The federal government had been making treaties with the Indians and moving them off their lands since the late 1700s, and in 1830 Congress had passed the Indian Removal Act that provided for the creation of an "Indian Country" and funds to transport eastern tribes across the Mississippi River for resettlement. By 1834 this land, known as the Indian Territory, was established in what is now Oklahoma, and most of the tribes native to Indiana had been forced from their land by the hostile removal efforts of the federal government. The Indian chiefs from various tribes further west who would become key players in the wars against white settlement—Sitting Bull, Geronimo, and Crazy Horse — were just being born during the early 1800s. It would be another twenty to thirty

years before they would rise to power and try to prevent the federal government from buying or taking their lands.

Overall, however, it was a love of freedom, fresh opportunity, and a desire for a better life that drew most people westward. Though the risks were great, the possible rewards seemed even greater. Hard work, good humor, and a strong faith were essential to survival. Somehow all the obstacles did not dissuade these pioneers who had a fortitude we can only admire in retrospect. It was hopes and dreams that propelled these brave people onward.

Keith Family Tree

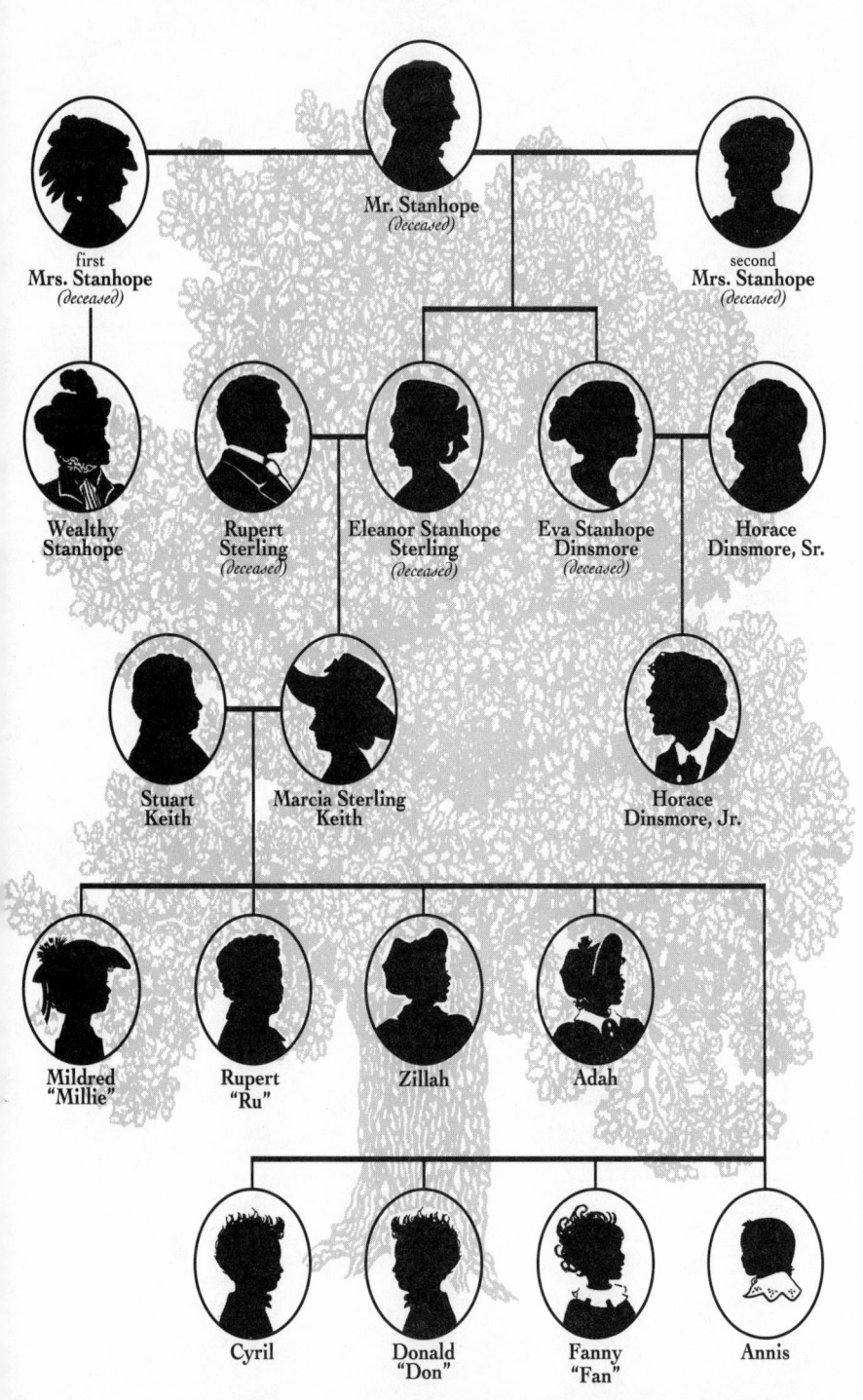

SETTING

*O*ur story begins in the 1830s in Lansdale, Ohio, a charming town, bustling with commerce and activity. Lansdale is home to the Keith family and was the birthplace of Millie Keith.

CHARACTERS

❧ THE KEITH HOUSEHOLD ❧

Stuart Keith—the father of the Keith family; a respected attorney-at-law.

Marcia Keith—the mother of the Keith family and the step-niece of Wealthy Stanhope.

The Keith children:
> **Mildred Eleanor ("Millie")**—age 12
> **Rupert ("Ru")**—age 11
> **Zillah**—age 9
> **Adah**—age 8
> **Cyril** and **Donald ("Don")**—age 7, twin boys
> **Fanny ("Fan")**—age 5
> **Annis**—an infant girl

Wealthy Stanhope—a woman in her mid-50s; Marcia's step-aunt who raised her from infancy; step-aunt to Horace Dinsmore, Jr.

Friends in Lansdale, Ohio

Annabeth Jordan, Beatrice Hartley and **Camilla Stone**—Millie's best girlfriends since childhood, known affectionately as "A, B, and C."

Frank Osborne—a childhood friend of Millie's, age 14.

Mrs. Hall—the matriarch of the wealthiest family in Lansdale, age 72.

Mr. Martin—a local schoolteacher.

Mr. and Mrs. Wiggles — friends of the Keith family.

Mr. Garlin — a friend of the family.

Friends in Pleasant Plains, Indiana

Mr. and Mrs. George Ward—old friends of Stuart Keith who live out on the prairie.

Mrs. Prior—the landlady of the Union Hotel.

Mrs. Lightcap—a widow who works as a laundress.
> **Gordon**—age 16, a blacksmith
> **Rhoda Jane**—age 14
> **Emmaretta**—age 8
> **Minerva**—age 7

Dr. and Mrs. Chetwood—the town physician and his wife.
> **William ("Bill")**—age 14
> **Claudina**—age 13

Mr. and Mrs. Grange—the bank president and his wife.

> **Lucilla**—age 14
>
> **Teddy**—age 9

Mrs. Gilligut—a widow.

Mr. and Mrs. Monocker—the owner of the local mercantile store and his wife.

> **York**—age 16
>
> **Helen**—age 15

Mr. and Mrs. Ormsby—a local businessman and his wife.

> **Wallace**—age 15
>
> **Sally**—age 5

Mr. and Mrs. Roe—local farmers.

> **Beth**—14
>
> **Joseph ("Joe")**—15

Celestia Ann Huntsinger—live-in housekeeper to the Keith family, age 17.

Reverend Matthew Lord—the new minister.

Damaris Drybread—a local teacher.

Mrs. Prescott—a widowed neighbor.

> **Effie**—age 7

Red Dog—an Indian man, member of the Potawatami tribe.

CHAPTER

1

Surprising News

Do not boast about tomorrow,
for you do not know what
a day may bring forth.

PROVERBS 27:1

Surprising News

*A*s the winter of 1833 melted away, the woods and gardens around Lansdale traded their blankets of snow for the glad rags of spring—a tinge of yellow-green spread over the woods, violets and anemones showed their pretty faces, rivulets danced and sang under apple, peach, and cherry trees in full bloom. Creation seemed to whisper, "Rejoice! He is risen!" And with the next breeze, "He is risen indeed!"

The girlish figure who slipped out the back door of the stately brick home in the center of town didn't seem to notice the whisper. She clutched a large, well-worn book to her chest, closed her eyes and leaned her head against the door.

Trust in the Lord…

"Millie!" A child's voice called, "Millie? Where are you?"

"Oh, not now!" Millie protested and ran across the garden to a fragrant cave beneath the arching lilacs. When she was sure that no one could see her behind the curtain of purple blooms, she sat down and opened the book.

"You know I am trying to acknowledge You, Lord," she prayed out loud. "But has there been a mistake? Something has gone wrong this time. I'm sure it has. Remember the verse Mamma gave me just yesterday? You must remember it, it's in *Your* book!" She flipped the Bible open. "Proverbs 3:5—"

Something cold touched her neck just as her finger found the place. Millie jumped, and whirled to find a little brown and white terrier looking up at her. He pressed his cold nose against her hand.

"What are you doing here, Wannago Stanhope?" Millie asked, scooping the pup into her arms. "I'm sure Aunty doesn't know you have escaped!" The dog whined and wagged his stub of a tail.

"Come on, I'll take you home." She tucked her Bible under one arm, the dog under the other, and walked across the garden to a wrought-iron gate; through the gate and another smaller garden to a tall brick house with vine-covered porches.

Windows opened to the wide porch across the back of the house, and a sweet voice was drifting from one of them.

"A mighty fortress is our God...," sang the voice.

"Aunt Wealthy?" Millie called.

"...a bulwark never failing!"

"Aunt Wealthy?" Millie called again.

"In here, dear," the voice sang from the parlor window. "Don't bother running around to the door. Step right in the window!"

Millie put her Bible on the sill, gathered up her skirts and petticoats and, after glancing around to make sure no one was watching, swung her legs up and over the window. Wannago bounced to the floor and started to bark up at a tiny, middle-aged lady who was perched like an ornamental vase on the large mantel above the fireplace. Her chintz gown was of her own peculiar design, and a scandalous flash of ankle showed each time she swung her little boot. She was fanning herself with a letter.

"Aunt Wealthy!" Millie exclaimed. "Whatever are you doing up there?"

"Spring cleaning," Wealthy said. "I was dusting the top of the mirror. Getting *down* is quite a different matter than getting up, isn't it? The stool tipped when I tried to step on it."

"How long have you been up there?" Millie asked, setting the stool upright.

"For one long letter and half a hymn," Wealthy said. "It is fortunate that I found a misplaced epistle from my nephew Horace Jr. on the mantel. It kept me good company for a half hour, but even accounts of the young Dinsmore's college life could not stretch much longer on the printed page. Wannago fled when I started to sing, and now here you are!"

Millie pushed the stool closer to the mantel and held up a hand to help her aunt down.

"Oh, Aunt Wealthy," Millie cried, as Wealthy's boot touched solid ground. "It's decided!"

"My child, what is it?" asked the older lady, dropping the letter to take the girl's hand and draw her to a seat on the sofa. "What is decided?"

Millie spoke with a determined effort to be calm.

"This morning at breakfast, Pappa told us—us children, I mean—he and Mamma had talked it over last night, and you know they have been praying about it, and..."

"And?" Wealthy clasped Millie's hand to her heart.

"We are going to move ... to ... to ... Pleasant Plains, Indiana."

"The frontier!" Wealthy gasped, sinking back on the couch.

"Just as soon as we can get ready. Isn't it marvelous?" Millie said, and burst into tears.

For a moment her listener was dumb with surprise, but it was not in Wealthy Stanhope's nature to witness distress without an effort to comfort and relieve.

"Now, now, Millie dear," the older woman said, drawing her niece close. She stroked the hand she held. "There will

be, perhaps, some adventures on the journey. I thought you yearned for adventure."

"I do! But I already know my adventure is completing my studies with Mr. Martin, and then Camilla and I will become the first female students to attend Tristan College. And then we're going to do something grand, something no woman has ever done before, something amazing! We will be doctors, or missionaries to some uncharted place on a faraway continent. We have it all planned! Aunty, I've been praying so hard about this, and I was sure God would find a way for me to stay in Lansdale. I don't want to leave my friends yet. Mamma even gave me a verse: 'Trust in the Lord with all your heart and lean not on your own understanding. In all your ways acknowledge him, and he will make your paths straight.'" She recited the words aloud, speaking earnestly as if she would carve the words into her heart. " 'He will make your paths straight.' Proverbs 3:6. I thought that meant if I trusted Him I could stay!"

Wealthy patted her hand in silence for a moment, then said, "You mustn't ignore verse 5, dear. 'Lean not on your own understanding.' Why, I remember," the tiny lady said, "when God changed my adventure. I was having a wonderful time living in a small room in Boston, helping servants just out of their indentures to find work, and teaching them to read the Scriptures. I was sure I would spend my whole life working with the Ladies Aid Society. Then I received word that my beloved sister's husband had died, and she herself was ill. I hurried home to care for her and her two-year-old daughter, but she was taken home to the Lord. As you can imagine, I was heartbroken and confused. My whole life had to change. I found myself with a child to raise—your mother. And look at what the Lord has done!

6

A spinster like me, with a niece as dear as a daughter and eight just-as-good-as grandchildren. God had a very special plan."

"Well, I *thought* He had one for me," Millie said. "Maybe I did something wrong and He changed His mind!"

"Nonsense," Aunt Wealthy said. "He isn't just sending the Keith clan. He is sending His very own Millie Keith, the bravest, most outspoken girl I know. There must be something very special He wants you to do in Pleasant Plains. Come along." She led the way into Millie's favorite place in the world, her well-stocked library. On any other day, Millie would have paused as she entered, breathing in the smell of leather bindings, book paste, and paper. If it were quiet, she would imagine that she could hear the voices of the books, a thousand adventures waiting to be discovered. But today, she followed Aunt Wealthy straight to the atlas that lay open on a table. Wealthy flipped to the new state of Indiana and traced an overland route with her finger.

"What roads there are will be very bad this time of year. Heavy wagons would get bogged down in the mud."

"Pappa said that, too. He said the best route would be up the Ohio and Erie Canal to Lake Erie, and around Michigan by ship."

"Very sensible," Wealthy agreed. Millie examined the maps while Aunt Wealthy pulled another book from the shelf.

"Tsk!" Wealthy said, flipping a page quickly. "Tsk, tsk!"

"What are you reading, Aunty?"

"Hmmmmm? Oh, just a little book written by a friend of mine. He spent some time in the territory that became the state of Indiana not too long ago. Oh dear!"

"What is it?" Millie asked. "What does it say?"

Millie's Unsettled Season

"Never mind," Wealthy said, replacing it on the shelf. "Perhaps I'll read it later. Would you like to take the maps to school with you today, to show your friends?"

"Oh, Aunty," Millie's eyes filled with tears again. "That's the worst part, the part I can't bear—no more school for me. There's too much sewing and packing to do between now and when we leave. But what's worse is that out on the frontier, there won't be school for me either—at least not like I have with Mr. Martin."

"No school?" Aunt Wealthy was speechless for a full minute. She brushed a tear from Millie's face. "You will still have books, and your father and mother—both educated people—will help you, and who knows but what you may end up with a better education than school can provide. I've found that the knowledge I've gained by my own efforts is often the most useful. Your skill with a needle and thread wasn't learned in school. You are a great help and comfort to your mother because of it."

"You're only saying that to cheer me up," Millie said.

"Nonsense," Aunt Wealthy said. "Since your mother had to let the servants go, you have been a great help to her. You not only help with the mending, you watch the little ones and—"

A blood-curdling scream brought Wealthy up from her seat, and they both raced to the window. A little girl with golden ringlets flying and wide blue eyes burst from the hydrangea bushes and raced to the porch, two seven-year-old red-headed boys right behind her.

Aunt Wealthy reached through the window and scooped the child into her arms.

"Fan! Cyril! Don!" Wealthy said, "Whatever are you doing?"

 8

"Playin'," Cyril said, quickly hiding something behind his back.

"We're going to the wild frontier!" Don yelled. "Wahoooo! I'm going to be a longhunter like Davy Crockett!"

"Me too," said Fan, not to be outdone. "I'm going to hunt bears and wildcats!"

"I'm not going to wear any clothes!" bellowed Don.

"Donald Keith!" scolded Millie. "You most certainly will wear clothes! And Cyril, what are you hiding behind your back?"

"His tomahawk," said Fan, wiggling out of Aunt Wealthy's arms. "He was going to scalp me!"

Millie held out her hand. Cyril reluctantly produced a twisted root that looked a bit like a hatchet.

"Cyril, you know better than to play with things like that," Millie said.

"You're not mother," Cyril replied.

"Now, I'm sure your mother would want you to obey Millie," Aunt Wealthy chided.

"Maybe," said Don, handing over the pretend tomahawk. "But I asked Mamma not to let her tell us what to do." He leaned close to Aunt Wealthy and whispered, "Millie pinches."

"Yeah," Cyril agreed. "She pinches *hard*."

"Only when you are very wicked," Millie said, flushing red, "and won't pick up your toys, or when you shout and wake the baby…or…or…try to scalp your little sister!"

Cyril skipped out of reach, and Don peeked around Aunt Wealthy's skirts.

"That's quite enough," Aunt Wealthy said firmly. "There will be no scalping today. It is a nasty habit, and quite unnatural."

"Indians scalp people," Don said.

"They did not until some wicked soldiers from France taught them to," Aunt Wealthy said. "A brave longhunter would never scalp his sister. He would lay down his life to protect her, because he would be a Christian gentleman and do just as Jesus would do."

"Was Jesus brave?"

"Very brave," Aunt Wealthy assured him. "He laid down His life for the world. It was the bravest thing anyone ever did. Now, did your Mamma say you could play in the back garden?"

"Yes," Cyril said.

"But first we had to find Millie," Don explained. "Mamma wants her. Rupert went with Pappa to the mercantile, and she needs someone to mind Zillah, Adah, and the baby."

"Zillah and Adah are playing dolls," Fan volunteered. "Yuck!"

"Why didn't you say Mamma needed me straightaway?" Millie asked, exasperated. Cyril poked out his tongue at her from the safety of Aunt Wealthy's skirt-tails. Millie's fingers itched to pinch him, but Aunt Wealthy's words were still echoing in her head: Christian gentlemen do just as Jesus would do. Of course Christian ladies should do the same. *Jesus, You didn't pinch Your younger brothers and sisters, did You?* Millie prayed. *Didn't they ever deserve it? I know James must have at least once, so You must know how I feel. I do want to be like You, but it's so hard! Please help me!* She shoved the offending fingers deep in the pockets of her apron.

"I think I'll take a walk around town," Aunt Wealthy said. "I always pray best when I'm walking, and I want to talk to my Lord. Come along." Millie followed her aunt but kept a safe distance from her brothers, just in case.

A few moments later, they said good-bye to Aunt Wealthy at her own gate. Millie stood for a moment and watched as her aunt, armed with a large cotton umbrella, marched briskly towards the business part of town. Could Aunt Wealthy be right? Did Jesus have something for her, Mildred Eleanor Keith, to do in Pleasant Plains? What possible difference could a twelve-year-old make in a frontier town?

CHAPTER

2

Preparing the Way

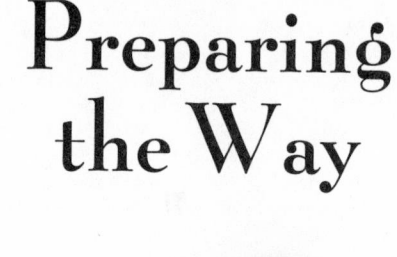

The Lord said… "Now then, you and all these people, get ready to cross the Jordan River into the land I am about to give to them."

JOSHUA 1:1-2

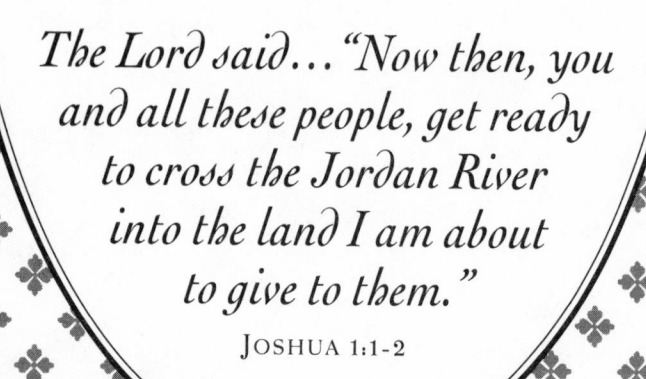

*M*illie tucked baby Annis into her bassinet and pulled the blanket up to her chin. Adah and Zillah had decided to go shopping with Pappa and Rupert. Don, Cyril, and Fan were playing explorers in the garden. Millie found her mother in the room off the kitchen where the washing was done. She stood for just one moment, watching her. Millie thought she was beautiful, even in her housedress with her sleeves rolled up and her arms deep in the big washtub of soapy water. Before Pappa had lost his money, the washer woman would have done the laundry; now the family had only the help of a cook. Once upon a time, Millie and her Mamma would have had time to read books and take walks with the children. But now, Millie watched the little ones while Mamma kept house. Washing alone for eight children took half the day! The clothes had to be boiled and scrubbed in the big wash bucket, wrung by hand and hung on the line. When they were dry, Millie would take them down and Mamma would iron them.

"Mamma?"

Marcia looked up with a smile. "Yes, Millie?"

"Mamma, did you know that we were going to move when you gave me that Bible verse?"

Marcia paused for a moment, wiping a stray hair from her face, and then said, "I suspected we might."

"How do you learn to trust the Lord?"

Marcia wiped her wet, soapy arms on her apron, then walked over to the table and pulled out a chair. "Sit down, Millie," she said.

Millie sat in the chair.

"Now, daughter, what is keeping you from tumbling to the floor?"

Millie looked surprised. "The chair!"

"Aren't you afraid it will let you fall?"

"Of course not. It's never let me fall before."

Marcia went back to the washtub. "I can trust in God because He has never let me fall. But everyone has a first time for trusting Him. Everyone has to learn for themselves that He loves them and won't let them fall. This is a good time to learn, my love."

"But it doesn't make sense! Didn't He know that Mr. Arnold would embezzle Pappa's money? That we would be poor and have to move?"

"It is hard. And a little scary. But you know, daughter, you are not the only one who has memory verses. Do you want to hear mine?"

Millie nodded.

"It's Hebrews 13:5: 'Make sure that your character is free from the love of money, being content with what you have; for he himself has said, "I will never desert you, nor will I ever forsake you," so that we confidently can say, "the Lord is my helper, I will not be afraid. What will man do to me?"' If Jesus was everything to me when I had servants and wore silks, Millie mine, how could He not be everything still, even if I am a servant and wear...suds?" She blew a bubble from the tips of her fingers. "Good heavens, what is that?"

Millie followed her gaze out the window. Wannago Stanhope was marching down the walk at the head of a comical caravan. Aunt Wealthy was right behind him, umbrella held high. Three small mountains of brown paper parcels followed her. Over the top of each parcel could be seen just a bonnet, and beneath them, boots skipping and hopping to avoid the puddles left by the recent rain.

"She's brought Annabeth, Bea, and Camilla!" Millie cried. "A, B, and C!"

"Run and open the gate," Marcia said, "while I clean up."

Millie flew down the steps and opened the gate, then led the way into the parlor. The girls laid the packages on the table.

"She wouldn't say a word," Annabeth said. "Not one word. But when Miss Wealthy Stanhope buys every fabric remnant in Lansdale, then you know that something is amiss."

"And so we came to find out what," Bea said practically.

"It isn't what we fear, is it, Millie?" Annabeth said. "It can't be. We've all been praying and praying…"

Millie's eyes stung, but she blinked hard. "My father and mother have been praying too, and they decided…the opportunities are just so good in Indiana…"

"Indiana!" Camilla collapsed in a heap on the ottoman. "Not possible. You can't! There should be a law against it!"

"A law against the Keiths moving to Indiana?" Bea shook her head.

"Of course not," Camilla said. "A law against the Keiths leaving Lansdale at all. I think we should sign a petition!"

"Annabeth, dear, are you quite all right?" Wealthy was looking at the tall, quiet girl.

Bea and Camilla stopped their chatter.

"We've always been together," Annabeth said. "How can you leave?"

Millie's throat felt tight. Even if she could have spoken, there was no word to express all the feelings jumbled inside. Not one word.

Millie's Unsettled Season

"Rump," Aunt Wealthy said, as if to sum up the situation. The girls glanced at one another.

"Pardon?" Bea said. "I'm afraid I didn't hear correctly."

"I mean this reminds me of my dear friend Hildegard Rump," Wealthy said. "Hilly and I have been friends forever. When the Lord called me to Boston to work with the Ladies Aid, we became even better friends. Somehow, we could share more of our hearts in letters than we could speaking face to face. And it was so wonderful to receive that letter every week. Dear Miss Hienden."

"Excuse me, Miss Stanhope, but who is Miss Hienden?" Camilla asked. "Weren't you speaking of a Miss Rump?"

"My goodness!" Wealthy said, flushing red. "Of course I meant Hienden! Hildegard Hienden. What was I thinking?"

The girls managed to contain their giggles until a squeak escaped Camilla; and then they all, including Aunt Wealthy, dissolved into laughter and tears.

"Aunt Wealthy!" Marcia said, entering the room. "You've come at last! And it looks like you have brought sunshine with you, as always." The girls burst into giggles again. "Hello, girls. You've been out shopping?"

"Yes, at every store in town," Aunt Wealthy replied. "So you're going to leave Lansdale, Marcia?"

"Yes, Aunty, and you. That's the worst of it."

"Not so fast. Who says that I'm to be left behind?"

"Aunt Wealthy! Do you mean it? Is it possible you could think of such a sacrifice?" cried Marcia.

"Pish-tosh," Aunt Wealthy said. "I have been sedentary for quite long enough. I can't give up the Stanhope homestead, as you very well know. But I have found a tenant for it. The young minister and his wife will be very happy to set up housekeeping, and they will take good care of my furniture and belongings for a year. I intend to see you all safely settled in Hoosier land before I return. It will be quite an importation of Buckeyes, won't it — all of us coming in one lot? Now to business," said Aunt Wealthy, attacking the parcels. "I'm going to help you, Marcia, in getting your tribe ready for their exodus out of this land of plenty into that Western Wilderness. Here are two or three dress patterns apiece for the little girls to travel in. I think they had better be made long-necked and high-sleeved, don't you?"

Millie had visions of her little sisters waddling like geese, their long necks stretched before them and arms held high.

Even Marcia looked slightly puzzled; then a light broke over her face. She was used to her aunt's odd way with words.

"I don't know," she said. "Wouldn't it make them look a little old-womanish? Low necks and short sleeves are prettier for children, I think, and they're used to it. Summer's coming on, too, and we must expect warm weather."

"It will be cool on the water."

"Yes, that's true," Marcia said. "I'll take your advice after all."

"Good. They'll be less likely to catch cold from any little exposure, and their necks and arms will be protected from the sun."

Before the Keiths' troubles had begun, Marcia would have engaged a seamstress or two, but now, her carefully managed household funds were just enough to pay the bills and the cook. It would take some weeks of very diligent work by three or four pairs of hands to accomplish what the mother deemed necessary in the way of preparing their wardrobe for the journey.

"Let me help with your sewing," Annabeth said.

"I'll help too," said Bea. "I know Mother will let me!" Annabeth and Bea were clever with their needles, and for the last two years the girls had worked together when they needed special gowns for parties or balls. Bea was especially clever at designing skirts that twirled when one danced, and Annabeth was simply the best at sewing lace.

"I think that would be wonderful," Marcia said. "You can keep Millie company."

Camilla looked down at her shoes. Everyone knew she was a disaster with a needle, and nothing less than frightening with a pair of scissors. Her mother ordered her gowns from Chicago, and Camilla was perfectly happy with that arrangement, as it left her free to pursue her studies.

Millie took her friend's hand. "I think we will need some help with baby Annis, too," she said.

"Really?" Camilla looked hopefully at Marcia.

"I know we will," Marcia said.

The girls agreed that they would be over after school the next day and then they said their good-byes.

Millie helped sort the fabric as Aunt Wealthy and Marcia discussed plans for the trip. Suddenly, the door burst open, letting in two little girls and a boy who was just a year younger than Millie. The girls were almost in tears, but the boy's blue eyes danced with mischief and fun.

"Softly, softly, children." Marcia said, looking up with a smile as they came in. "The baby is sleeping. Rupert, eleven is quite old enough to begin to act in a more gentlemanly way, don't you think?"

"Yes, Mamma, I beg your pardon. Yours too, Aunt Wealthy. I didn't know till this moment that you were here."

"Now, Adah, Zillah, what is this about?"

"Ru says we'll have to live in wigwams like the Indians and eat raw fish with their eyeballs still in," Zillah said. Adah, who hated fish, started to cry.

"I'm sure we will have bread and butter," Millie said, hugging her little sister, and glaring at her brother.

"Rupert, my son, was it quite truthful to tell your sisters such things?"

"I was only making fun," he answered, trying to turn it off with a laugh, but blushing as he spoke.

"I never object to innocent fun. But amusement is too dearly bought at the sacrifice of truth," Marcia said.

Zillah and Adah caught sight of the dress fabric and instantly forgot wigwams and fish. "Are we getting new dresses, Mamma? Can mine be blue? Will you sew lace on my collar? Will we be beautiful?"

"Beautiful? Why, I have the most beautiful girls in the world! And my wife is the most beautiful of all!" said Stuart Keith, who stood in the doorway, Fan tucked under his left arm and Cyril and Don dangling by their suspenders from his right hand. "Look what I found lurking in the bushes. A pack of wild children. May I keep them, dear?"

"If you promise to wash them and teach them their manners," Marcia said, rising to kiss her husband.

"On my word, I will." He sent the boys and Fan to wash up, then tossed his hat onto the hat rack. "Hello, Aunt Wealthy. Have you heard the news?"

"That you are going to Indiana, Stuart? Yes, I've heard something about it," Wealthy said with a twinkle in her eye. "Not content to live in this civilized and cultured town, are you?"

"Lawyers are not so plentiful there, and as more folks move in, legal services will be in great demand. I plan to open my own practice. And land is cheap. I'll invest in a portion of it and hope to see it increase in value as the town grows. However," his voice grew solemn, "it will mean the sundering of some very dear ties here."

"Do you know," Marcia asked, smiling at Wealthy, "that since you left us this morning something has happened that takes away more than half the pain of leaving Lansdale? Aunt Wealthy is coming along!"

"Truly?" Stuart pulled Wealthy from her seat and waltzed her across the floor. "The Lord has blessed us!"

They were interrupted by a summons from Mary, the cook. She was always prim and very discreet, and she would have disapproved of the display, if it had been proper to notice it at all.

"Thank you, Mary," Marcia said. "Will you set an extra place for Aunt Wealthy?"

Millie loved suppertime. She could pretend that nothing had happened and that life was just the same as it had always been. The family gathered at the table in the soft glow of oil lamps. Mary served them quietly and then left.

Stuart bowed his head and led the family in a prayer. Then the meal began with the sweet ting of silver on china.

"So what has my family been up to today?" Stuart asked.

"We told Mr. and Mrs. Wiggles that we were moving to Indiana," Fan said. "She said she would pray for us."

"Mr. Wiggles said he would pray for the Indians," Don volunteered.

"Very kind of him, I'm sure," Stuart said dryly. "But most of the tribes have been removed. They have gone to live west of the Mississippi, where there is more land and fewer white men. There is just one tribe left in Indiana."

"The Wotapotamies?" Wealthy asked.

"The Potawatamies, yes."

"A fascinating people," Aunt Wealthy said, without pausing to correct herself. "The Potawatamies fought very fiercely against the British. They were allied with the French. Then they fought as allies with the British against the Americans."

"Did the bad soldiers teach them to scalp peoples?" Fan asked, eyes as big as saucers.

"Well...yes," Aunt Wealthy said. "During the French and English war. But that was a long time ago, child."

"Pappa," Rupert asked, "what about Black Hawk? They say he is out of prison. Couldn't the Indians come back?"

Millie put her fork down. She remembered the talk in school about Black Hawk, a fierce Sauk warrior. He believed that the Indians had been cheated out of their land and tricked into signing contracts they did not understand. He gathered a band of five hundred Sauk and Fox warriors. Along with their women and children, they came back across the Mississippi to the lands that had once been their home and fought with soldiers of the United States government. When Black Hawk was finally defeated, it was a terrible massacre. Soldiers shot down women and children, killing even tiny babies. Black Hawk's followers were wiped out. Millie remembered Mamma crying when she read the accounts in the paper.

"Black Hawk has lost his followers," Stuart said. "The Sauk tribe looks to Keokuk now, a reasonable man who wants peace. Mr. Wiggles was right. We should pray for the Indians."

3

A Big Decision

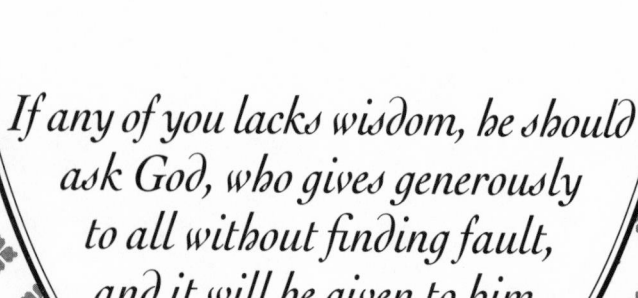

*If any of you lacks wisdom, he should
ask God, who gives generously
to all without finding fault,
and it will be given to him.*

JAMES 1:5

s the weeks passed, Millie was grateful for her friends' company in the afternoons as they sewed. Their conversation almost took the sting out of leaving Mr. Martin's class. Millie had begun to think, under Mr. Martin's tutelage, that she might want to be a teacher herself one day. His classroom was a botanical and zoological wonder, with specimens and samples of all kinds. When Bea complained that girls should not be expected to learn mathematics, history, Latin, and Greek as the boys were, Mr. Martin had removed his spectacles, polished them carefully, then perched them once again on his beak-like nose.

"I suppose you adhere to the wisdom of young ladies studying only music, drawing, embroidery, and French, Miss Hartley?"

"Why, yes," Bea answered. "Although truthfully, I would rather dispense with the French altogether."

Mr. Martin shook his bald head, then picked up the flower they had been sketching. "The lily is a work of art, don't you agree?"

"Of course," Bea said. "It's beautiful."

"And beautifully and thoughtfully made. Do you realize that each and every part of this flower has a purpose?"

"Yes," Bea agreed. "We have been studying the lily."

"You are beautifully and thoughtfully made also," Mr. Martin said. "And every part of you has a purpose. As God saw fit to give you a good brain, I expect you to use it. There is room in that lovely head for embroidery and mathematics, Miss Hartley!"

Camilla thrived in the classroom setting, and after school each day as the girls sewed, she described the lessons to

Millie's Unsettled Season

Millie, pouring over her notes until Bea and Annabeth begged her to stop. The conversations and company were very dear to Millie, since she wanted to spend every minute possible with her friends, but the long hours beside Mamma and Aunt Wealthy while they were alone proved more useful in getting the work done.

The Keith house began to look less and less like home, as trunks were packed and belongings sorted into those that would travel with the family, and those that would be shipped ahead. Wagons were loaded and sent away, leaving the house with empty corners and echoes in the halls.

"Have you any cord, Marcia?" asked Aunt Wealthy one morning while they worked together in the sewing room.

"Yes," Marcia answered, turning to her work basket. "Why, what has become of it? I had two or three pieces here. And that paper of needles has disappeared. Millie, did you use them?"

"The children were here half an hour ago," Millie said. "I remember seeing Donald looking into your basket."

"Run out and see what they have done with the cord," Marcia said. "Ask after the needles too. We don't want them turning up in the wrong place."

Millie hesitated in the empty hall, listening for sounds to tell her where the children were. Little voices were prattling in the garden near at hand. Stepping to the door she saw Cyril and Don seated on the grass, busy with a kite Rupert had made for them.

"What are you doing?" she asked, going nearer.

"Making a longer tail."

"Where did you get that piece of string?"

The only answer was a guilty look on the two grubby faces.

28

A Big Decision

"Oh, I know! You took it from Mamma's work basket. And now Aunt Wealthy needs it, but you've spoiled it entirely. Don't take things without leave. Did you take a paper of needles too?"

"No, we didn't," Don said. "You always think we are the ones causing trouble."

"So you didn't see the paper of needles?"

"We *saw* it," said Don, "but Fan took it."

"Yeah, she was bothering us," added Cyril.

I will not pinch. No matter how much they deserve it, Millie said to herself. She shoved her hands in her pockets and went in search of her little sister. She found Fan sitting in her little garden, the empty needle paper lying near. Fan was sitting cross-legged, her chin resting on her fist, staring at the ground.

"Fan," said Millie as she picked the paper up, "what have you done with the needles?"

"Sowed them in the ground," said Fan, smoothing the dirt with her little rake. "When they grow into baby porkypies, we'll have lots of needles! I have to watch careful, or the porkypies will get away."

"Porcupines," Millie corrected her.

"Will you help me pluck them, Millie?" Fan asked, holding up her chubby hands. "They'll prick me!"

"No they won't. Needles do not grow into porcupines. Who told you that story, silly little puss? Never mind, I can guess. Show me where you put them."

"I put them in the ground, round and round."

Millie picked up a stick and poked about in the fresh earth for a minute or two.

Millie's Unsettled Season

"This is as hopeless as looking for needles in a haystack," she said. "Come on, I'm sure you can play with Zillah. She is making a dress for her doll."

She went back into the house with the report of the hapless fate of the missing needles, but the boys were there before her. They'd washed their faces and their hands up to the wrists and slicked down their hair. Millie was sure she could smell just a hint of rose water.

"We didn't think, Mamma," pleaded Donald, penitently holding out the ruined cord. "We're very sorry."

"Very, very sorry," Cyril said earnestly.

Marcia leaned over and gave him a kiss. "My boys must learn to think. And they must not take mother's things without asking. Now run along and try to be good children."

"Mother, I do think you're a little too easy with them," Millie said with frustration. "They've been telling Fan terrible tales to keep her out of their way, and they do know better than to take your cord."

"Perhaps," Marcia said, "but if I make a mistake, it is far better to do so on the side of mercy than of severity. And they did apologize."

"That's true," Aunt Wealthy said. "What have they told Fan this time?" she asked.

Millie related the story of Fan's baby porcupines, and she couldn't help laughing along with her mother and aunt.

"We can't do without needles, I'm afraid," said Marcia when Millie was finished. "Will you run to the store and get a new paper, Millie?"

Millie put on her bonnet. She felt almost guilty escaping into the beautiful day. If it hadn't been for the fact that she would miss her afternoon reading, she would have been perfectly happy.

A Big Decision

News had traveled, and everyone in town knew that the Keiths were moving. People greeted Millie as she walked along the street and asked her about her family and their preparations. Millie gave each an answer and a smile. As she turned a corner onto Main Street, she almost ran into Frank Osborne, the boy who sat in front of her in class.

"Millie, what a surprise!" he said, jumping aside. He recovered his balance and took her hand in a friendly greeting. Millie felt her cheeks grow warm. Frank was the smartest boy in school, and a year ahead of Millie. She greatly enjoyed talking about books and history with him. Bea, Camilla, and Annabeth had started to tease her about the amount of time Frank spent sitting under the tree in the schoolyard, reading with Millie.

"The news of your moving has come as a great shock to the whole class," Frank said, dropping her hand. "Can it really be true? You are going to Indiana?"

"Yes, to the land of the Hoosier, wild Indians, and wolves," Millie said gaily. "Don't you envy me?"

"I envy those that go with you," he answered. "And I wonder who will challenge me in the spelling bee now. You won't forget old friends, Miss Millie?"

"No, no indeed, Frank," she said heartily. "I won't forget. But good-bye. I must purchase my supplies and hurry home," and with a nod and smile she left him. Millie didn't look back, but she caught a reflection in the glass door of the shop as it swung open—a ghostly picture of Frank standing on the walk where she had left him, his hands in his pockets.

Millie had just finished paying for the needles when a woman called her name.

"Mildred Keith!"

"Good morning, Mrs. Hall," Millie said politely. The Halls were the wealthiest family in town, good Christians, and always ready to help anyone in need.

"I am so glad I ran into you," Mrs. Hall said. "I have been meaning to speak to your mother, but I have been too busy to get by. Will you walk with me to my carriage?"

"Of course," Millie said, taking Mrs. Hall's package, and walking beside her.

"Millie," the elderly lady said, "I have been speaking to your teacher, Mr. Martin. He has told me how much you value your education, and how sorry he is to lose you as a pupil. He thinks very highly of you, and of your possibilities, my dear. I've heard of the difficulties your father had. I have had some difficulties of my own lately—Dr. Brent has said that I must not strain my heart. I was thinking I could get a girl to stay with me, to help with the light lifting and accompany me on walks." Millie's heart skipped a beat.

"Perhaps it would be too great a sacrifice for your dear parents. But you could continue your education, and they would know you were in a good Christian home. What do you think?"

"I…I truly don't know what to think, Mrs. Hall. It's such a kind offer! But…"

"Oh, I know the decision will be up to your parents," Mrs. Hall said with a smile. "I simply thought you might put in a good word for me."

"Thank you, Mrs. Hall. I will speak to Mamma about it." Millie watched the carriage roll away.

Stay in Lansdale! Was it possible? She started to walk toward home, but suddenly stopped, tucked the paper of needles into her sash, and ducked into the hedge beside the road. She ran until her breath was coming in gasps, up the

hill to the old oak that grew on top. She pulled herself up until she was standing on the lowest branch, petticoats and all, and hugged the trunk of the tree. She hadn't climbed the oak since she was Zillah's age. Somehow the rough bark against her face was comforting.

Lansdale stretched across the valley before her, lovely brick homes, tree-shaded streets, white church steeples pointing at the sky. Lansdale where everyone knew her, where her friends lived. Where she could finish her studies with Mr. Martin, and then attend college.

"Could this be Your plan?" Millie prayed out loud. "Could You want me to stay after all? But what about Mamma and Pappa? I don't know what to do!" Millie sighed. "I am willing to trust in You. But please, show me what I should do!"

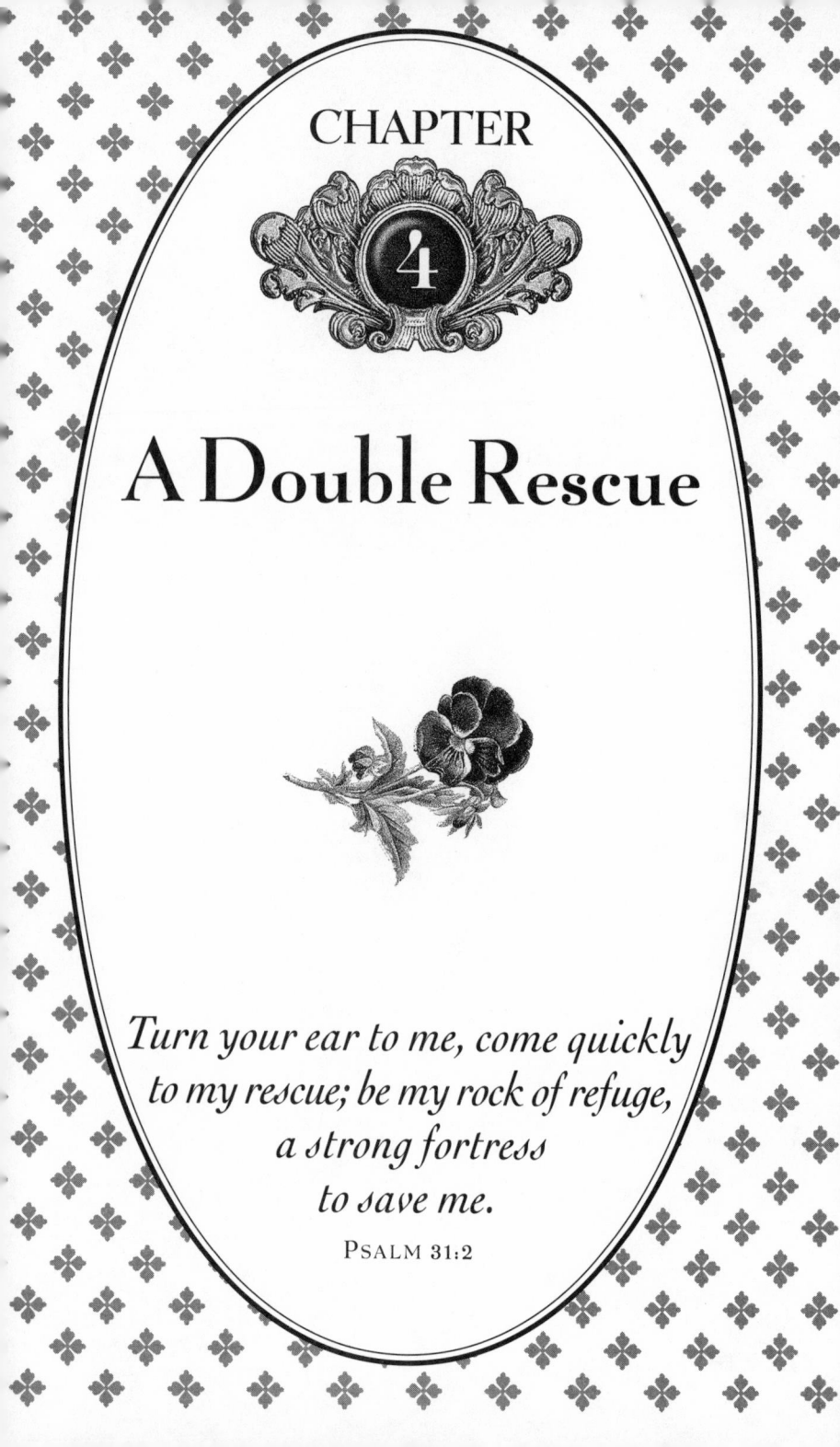

CHAPTER

4

A Double Rescue

*Turn your ear to me, come quickly
to my rescue; be my rock of refuge,
a strong fortress
to save me.*

PSALM 31:2

A Double Rescue

*M*illie's steps were a little slower as she made her way home. Lansdale had looked dear and bright on her walk to the store, when she had known that she would be leaving. Now the future was not as certain. How could she stay with her friends and continue her education while her dear Mamma and Pappa traveled to a strange place? And the children!

She delivered the needles and cord, and set to pulling out a seam that had gone wrong.

"Mamma, how does God answer you when you pray?"

"Well," Marcia replied, snipping the end of her thread. "Sometimes He talks to me as I am reading my Bible—a verse just stands out. At other times, He brings a Scripture that I have memorized to mind. Sometimes He speaks to me through your father, who is a very wise and godly man. Sometimes it takes a long time, and sometimes," she exchanged a knowing look with Wealthy, "it doesn't. He seems to have answered Pappa's prayer about the house already."

"He has?" Millie set her sewing down.

"Pappa just sent word. Mr. Garlin's nephew is willing to buy our house! But we have to be out by the first of June—in just two more weeks!"

Millie looked at the pile of fabric waiting to be turned into dresses, pants, and shirts. "Couldn't God have taken a little longer, Mamma? How can we possibly finish in time?"

"When you ask God for help, sometimes you get a surprise," Aunt Wealthy said. "Just think about the children of Israel, when they left Egypt. The Red Sea before them and Pharaoh's army behind them. When they cried out for

God to save them, I'm sure they didn't expect Him to tell them to march right through the sea! When God has a plan, He makes a way!" She stood and gestured, as if by a wave of her hand she would part the calico and chintz and they would sort themselves into neatly sewn garments.

"The Israelites still had to do the marching," Marcia said practically. "And we still have to do the sewing. But I know He will help us get this done. I am determined to finish Adah's dress today."

The words had scarcely left her lips when there came a loud crash and scream from the hall, and the sound of tumbling and rolling.

Scissors, thimbles, and fabric flew in every direction as Marcia, Millie, and Aunt Wealthy sprang up all at once.

Millie rushed into the hall and almost tripped over Cyril, who was lying at the foot of the stairs, amidst the fragments of a large pitcher.

"You kilt him, Fan!" Don cried, looking down from the landing. "He's dead!" Fan, sitting halfway up the stairs and completely drenched with water, started sobbing hysterically.

"Cyril's dead!"

"No, he ain't," said Cyril, sitting up. "Mamma, I didn't mean to. Ow!" The hand he raised to his head came away bloody. A stream of blood poured down the side of his face. "Oh, I can't stop it!"

"Shhhh. We'll take care of it," said his mother, taking his head in her hands and holding the lips of the wound together. "A basin of cold water, Millie, quick! And be careful not to step on any sharp shards. Aunty, there is sticking plaster in the worktable drawer. Hush, Don. Don't cry anymore, Fan; Cyril isn't hurt too badly. Mother will soon make it all right."

Millie brought the basin, water, and a clean cloth, and Aunt Wealthy the plaster. Marcia cleaned the wound and then pressed hard on it to stop the bleeding.

"Come along, Fan," Millie said, as her mother commenced bandaging Cyril's head. "Let's get you into a dry frock."

Cyril was still sniffling when they returned. His head was wrapped in a clean white bandage.

"Now, Cyril," Aunt Wealthy said, taking off her brooch. "That's enough of that." She pinned her brooch on the front of his bandage. "There! You look just like a Sheik of Araby."

Don eyed the headband enviously.

"Don't even think of throwing yourself down the stairs, Don," Millie said. "Aunty hasn't any more brooches on her."

"Now, how did this happen?" Marcia asked.

"Why—why," said Cyril, "Fan wanted to wash her hands cause she'd been digging in the garden."

"Yeah, digging in the garden," Don echoed. Millie made a mental note to check the garden for buried valuables.

"Her hands was all dirty and there wasn't any water in the pitcher, so we brung it down and got it full and I was carrying it up and my foot tripped and... and I fell down with it and knocked Fan over 'cause she was behind me. And I couldn't help it. Could I, Don?"

"You couldn't," Don agreed. "Fan couldn't neither."

"And he's got a bad hurt on his head," put in Fan pityingly. "Poor Cyril!"

"Yes, he's punished enough, I think," said Marcia, adjusting his bandage. "His intentions seem to have been good; but next time you want water, dears, come tell

Mother or sister Millie. And now you must play quietly for a time, for Mother has lots and lots of work to do."

"Well, the morning's gone," said Millie, "and half the afternoon, too—wasted by the pranks of those children. I hope they've finished up their business for today." When Annabeth, Camilla and Bea knocked on the door a few moments later, Millie felt as if reinforcements had arrived just in time.

Camilla took the younger children in hand, promising to read to them from Millie's new copy of *Ivanhoe* as she led them upstairs, while Bea and Annabeth set about cutting fabric to Aunt Wealthy's patterns. Bea chattered happily about the boys at school and the plans for a summer dance in the town square. She had three months to convince her mother to let her stay up late for the moonlight dance. Millie shook her head at her friend's plans.

"I'll be thirteen by the dance," Bea said. "I'm sure Mother will let me stay up. That's practically grown!" The grand ballrooms and gowns Bea spun in the air certainly made the time pass quickly, and it didn't seem to hinder their sewing at all. Even Annabeth joined the fun, helping Bea imagine the colors and fabrics of the gowns, until Bea looked up from her stitches. "Oh, Millie," she said, "do they ever have dances in Indiana?"

"I'm sure they must," Millie said. But she wasn't sure at all. *It's not as civilized*, Pappa had said. *And we may have to do without a few comforts we are used to. But we will be a part of something grand—building a town!* "Though they may not be as grand as the dances in Lansdale."

"I'm sure they're not. Honestly, Millie, you are as brave as King David, or at least one of his mighty men," Bea said.

"Leaving everything you know and hold dear, traveling to a distant land fraught with peril."

"I'm sure that's making her feel much better, Bea," Annabeth said with a touch of sarcasm. "Knowing that Indiana is not only fraught with peril, but is devoid of dances."

"Oh, I'm sorry, Millie," Bea said. "Perhaps…perhaps you can dance with the savages. They wear dresses made of deerskin, don't they? I wonder how you sew that. It seems to me that it would itch."

"Honestly, Bea, you should pay more attention in class," Annabeth said. "Mr. Martin taught us all about Indians last fall. Cured doeskin is soft enough for babies' clothes. And they make it beautiful by sewing on beads and dyed porcupine quills. Weren't you paying the least bit of attention?" Bea shook her brown curls.

"I don't think your velvet gown will itch," Millie said, changing the subject before her friends started to bicker. The girls discussed Lansdale activities for the rest of the afternoon, and somehow managed to accomplish more in two hours than even Marcia had thought possible.

When Millie showed her friends to the door and said good-bye, her heart ached. She wanted to tell them all about Mrs. Hall's offer, to ask what they would do. Or simply to say, I will need a gown for the ball too, Bea! I'm not going to Indiana after all! But she knew she should talk to her Mamma and Pappa first. She shut the door behind her friends and went back to the parlor. Mamma had started hemming Adah's dress, and the needle fairly flew in her quick fingers. Millie picked up her own sewing. How could she tell Mamma? What could she say? Suddenly shrieks and wails once again brought the three to their feet.

"What now?" Marcia exclaimed. They followed the squeals to a door on the second floor.

"Tsk," said Aunt Wealthy when the door was opened, "what a dreadful mess!"

Every chair was out of place and turned on its side, the bed-clothes were all tumbled, and bits of paper littered the carpet.

Howls and grunts were coming from a large oak bureau that was tipped forward, leaning precariously against a chair. Four skinny little legs stuck out of the lowest drawer. Don's boots were kicking and he was grunting like a penned bull. Cyril's one visible foot was still, but the banshee-like howl had to be coming from his throat.

"Ouch," someone yelled, "you kicked me!" and then, "Shhhh."

The grunts stopped.

"I think someone's out there," Cyril said. "You're gonna be in really big trouble. Ouch!"

"I'm not going to be in trouble. You are!" said Don. "You're the one that wanted to take the coach. I told you we shoulda taken the horses."

"Shhhh," Cyril said again. "Hello? Is anybody there?"

Marcia and Aunt Wealthy answered by lifting the bureau upright. Millie pulled the boys out of the drawer.

"Thank you, Mamma," Cyril said.

"What were you doing in the drawer?" Aunt Wealthy asked.

"We were on our way to rescue Rowena," said Cyril, straightening his shirt. "I told him we shoulda taken the horses instead."

"Horses?" Aunt Wealthy asked, looking around.

"Aw, he means the chairs," Don motioned to the upside-down chairs. "We're tired of ridin' them."

"And where is Rowena?" Marcia asked, checking the upper drawers.

"Locked up in the tower." Cyril motioned to the wardrobe with his thumb. "Safe and sound."

Millie unlocked the wardrobe. Fan was sitting quietly in the back corner, chin on her hand.

"Oh, Fan," Millie said. "How long have you been in there?"

"Since Camilla left," the little girl said. "Cyril and Don said I had to wait for them to rescue me. I was getting tired of waiting."

"The naughty boys!" cried Millie. "Mother, I do think they ought to be punished."

"We didn't hurt her," Don muttered, hanging his head. "It was just a game. And we didn't mean to tumble the bureau over. Did we, Cyril?"

"You might have been hurt very badly yourselves if the chair had not been where it was," his mother said gravely. "I am very thankful for your escape, and you must never do such things again. Especially never lock each other into a wardrobe or closet," she added, sitting down and drawing Fan to her lap. Aunt Wealthy and Millie restored the contents of the bureau drawers, which the boys had unceremoniously tossed upon the carpet.

"Why, Mamma?"

"Because it is very dangerous. Your little sister might have died for lack of air."

"Died dead?"

Marcia nodded gravely. Don's eyes filled with tears.

"I won't ever, ever do it again," he said tremulously.

"Of course not. I don't believe my boys would be so mean and cowardly as to hurt anyone smaller or weaker than themselves," Marcia said.

"But we didn't hurt her, Mamma," Cyril said.

"I think you hurt her feelings very much."

Fan nodded. "I think I need a bandage," she said, pointing to her heart. "Right there."

"Oh," Marcia said. "Bandages won't help there. But kisses will." She drew Fan into her ams and kissed her.

Cyril considered the scene with folded arms.

"I'm sorry, Fan," he said at last. "Here," he said as he pulled the brooch from his headband and pinned it over her heart. "Now don't be a cry-baby."

"Now, I want you to pick up this room, children, and keep out of mischief for the rest of the day. Millie will watch over you while you set it right. And I expect you to do a good job."

"Yes, Mamma," Don said.

Cyril nodded.

"I must go back to my work," Marcia said, following her aunt, who had already left the room.

Millie was congratulating herself on the fact that she had not pinched Cyril or Don even once since her conversation with Aunt Wealthy weeks ago, and was rarely even tempted to anymore, when she came upon her treasured copy of *Ivanhoe*, tumbled in a blanket. The pages were folded and creased, and one, a picture of Rebecca at the stake, was torn down the middle.

"You naughty boys!" Millie said. "Look what you have done to my book! I think you should get spankings all around."

"We wanted to know what happened next," Cyril said. "I tried to read it to Don and Fan, but the words were too hard."

"Well, you're not going to find out now," Millie said, closing the book carefully, and pressing the covers together to straighten the pages, and gripping it hard to keep her fingers busy. "I'm putting it away."

"You can't just put it away," Cyril said. "What happens to Ivanhoe? Does he get his castle back?" His freckles were standing out against his white face.

"I most certainly can put it away, Cyril Keith," Millie said adamantly. "It is my book, and you have mistreated it! You didn't even say you were sorry! I'm putting it away for good."

Fan crept close to Millie and slipped her arms around her.

"I'm sorry, Millie," she whispered.

"Me, too," Don said.

"Well, I'm not," Cyril said, wiping a tear from his cheek. "I'm not sorry at all. You are the meanest ol' sister in the whole world!"

"Pride goeth before a fall," Millie quoted.

"What's that s'posed to mean?" Cyril asked.

"Nothing to you," Millie said, and pinched him.

It was evening. Two candles burned on the sitting room table, and beside it sat Millie and her mother, still busy with their needles. The rest of the family were in bed and Aunt Wealthy had gone to her own home long ago.

"What are you thinking, daughter?"

Millie's Unsettled Season

Millie realized that her hands were resting in her lap.

"I am wondering how you put up with so much trouble from the children," Millie said.

Marcia smiled. "I had a lot of practice with their older sister," she laughed. "You were just as mischievous as they are, Millie mine. As soon as you could crawl, you spent your days pulling tablecloths down, breaking, tearing, climbing fences and trees, and even getting out of windows onto roofs. And you had a perfect mania for tasting every-thing that could possibly be put in your mouth—soap, can-dles, camphor, lye, medicines, whatever you could lay your hands on. I was in constant fear for your life."

"Poor, dear mother," Millie said. "How can I ever hope to repay you for your patient love and care?"

"You have been well worth all the trouble. I cannot tell you how much I enjoy the company and confidence of my eldest daughter. However, it is time to put up your work for tonight. You've had a long day."

Millie set her work aside and started to leave the room, but turned back.

"Mamma, I am so disgusted with myself. I know I couldn't sleep!"

"Why, Millie, what's wrong?"

Millie explained about the torn book and her harsh words with Cyril.

"I'm sorry about your book," Marcia said. "I didn't know they had caused such destruction."

"It was easy to forgive Don and Fan because they said they were sorry, and I know they meant it," Millie said. "But I haven't forgiven Cyril yet. It wasn't wrong to be angry, I know. But I haven't forgiven him, and that is a sin. The Bible says, 'Be angry, but do not sin. Do not let the sun go down while you are still angry.' The sun has been down a long time, and I am still so angry! I don't know what to do!" Millie knelt and laid her head in her mother's lap.

Marcia stroked her daughter's hair for a moment before she spoke. "You were angry because Cyril tore a book that was very precious to you," she said.

Millie nodded.

"I think you need to give your book away," said Marcia.

"Not to Cyril!" Millie sat up.

"No," said her mother smiling. "Not to Cyril. Give it to Jesus. Then ask yourself if He would forgive Cyril for tearing His book. If you give Him the things that are precious to you, you will be surprised what He can do with them."

"Mamma, that's not all." Millie's voice didn't want to work, but she forced herself to explain how she had pinched her brother.

"You have taken the first step, Millie mine," said Marcia. "Sins have a hold on you if you keep them hidden inside. The Bible tells us to confess our sins to each other and pray for each other so that we may be healed. I am glad you confessed to me. Now would you like me to pray for you?"

"Yes, Mamma."

"Dear Heavenly Father," her mother prayed, "I thank You that Millie's heart is tender toward You. And I ask You to help her control her temper, and not to pinch anymore."

"I'm sorry, Jesus," Millie said. "I'm sorry I wasn't like You, and I'm sorry I was prideful, and I'm sorry I hurt Cyril."

"You know He forgives us as soon as we ask, don't you, dear?" Marcia whispered.

"Yes, Mamma. And I will apologize to Cyril in the morning."

"Goodnight, Millie."

Millie lit a stub of a candle and kissed her mother good-night. When she reached her room, she took the copy of *Ivanhoe* from the top shelf and found a fresh quill on her desk. She uncorked the inkwell, dipped the nib, and marked out her own name from the bookplate. Then carefully, with her best penmanship, she wrote in "Jesus" instead. She blotted the letters carefully and left the book open for the ink to dry as she knelt beside her bed.

"Jesus," she prayed, "Mamma said that You could do amazing things if I give You the things that are precious to me. So...I want You to have this book. You can do anything You want with it. And...and I want to give You my hopes and dreams, too. I want You to have my future, Jesus. Please, please do something amazing with it!"

Millie crawled into her bed and pulled the blankets up to her chin. *So that's what answered prayers are like*, she thought. Because she knew, just as certainly as if someone had whispered it in her ear, that Jesus wanted her to go to Indiana—even though it would tear her heart as surely as Cyril had torn her book.

CHAPTER

5

The Journey Begins

*This calls for patient endurance
and faithfulness on the part
of the saints.*

REVELATION 13:10

The Journey Begins

The mood of the small group of family and friends gathered on Aunt Wealthy's vine-covered front porch on the last day of May was an odd mixture of excitement and tears. Millie was sure she knew exactly how the children of Israel had felt when they faced the Red Sea. She swallowed hard, and tried to smile at her friends.

"The girls do look sweet, Millie," said Bea as she adjusted the bow on Zillah's bonnet. Millie had to agree. Adah and Zillah were neat and clean in their new travel outfits. Millie had sewn Adah's herself, and Bea and Annabeth had finished Zillah's. "Do you suppose there will be shops in Pleasant Plains? I expect the fashions will be a bit backward—"

"Who cares about the fashions?" Camilla said. "What are you going to do about your studies? And are you taking books to read on the way?"

"I expect there will be shops," Millie said. "And I have packed my own books to read, though who knows how much time I will have, as I am minding the children." Millie bit her lip. Even if there were no shops, no parties, and not the slightest hint of fashion, she knew she could get by. But her friends! What would she do without them? Without Bea to help with dresses, without Annabeth to understand her heart before she even spoke, without Camilla to read sonnets?

"I wish I were taking you all with me!" Millie said. Annabeth took her hand and squeezed it.

"Is the stage late, Pappa?" Rupert asked.

"Just a little. Don, get down off that trellis."

"But Pappa, I want to be the first one to see it!"

Millie's Unsettled Season

"I think we can arrange that without pulling down Aunty's vines." He swung Don up onto his shoulders. "Let's take a little walk down the street."

He strode off with Zillah and Adah on each side, and Cyril and Fan dancing along behind.

"You have nappies for the baby?" Aunt Wealthy asked, for the third time.

"Yes, Aunty dear. I have everything we will need."

"I can't believe you are really going," Annabeth said to Millie. "Remember, you promised to write us every week."

"And send the letters to you by turns," Millie nodded, "so that you can read them together. The first will go to Camilla." Camilla just nodded. There were tears in her sweet blue eyes, and Millie knew she was fighting to keep them from falling.

"It's coming!" Ru was the first one to run back up the street. "The coach is coming!"

Millie turned to look one last time at the beautiful brick home she was leaving. That window with the morning glory vine was Mamma's room—and that's where Millie had been born. The nursery, the kitchen that was filled with gingerbread smells at Christmas, the dining room where Pappa always led the prayers...Millie felt an arm slip around her waist.

"It was a beautiful home," her mother whispered. "God blessed me with eight children there. And the same God that blessed me there will be with us wherever He leads us." Millie and her mother turned back together, just as four prancing steeds swept around the corner, and swaying and rolling, the coach dashed up to the gate.

The driver drew in rein, and the guard sprang from his lofty perch, threw open the door, and let down the steps.

The Journey Begins

Wannago stood on his hind legs and spun in place, afraid he would be left behind, but Aunt Wealthy opened her carpet-bag and he jumped in. She zipped it almost shut with just his nose peeking out.

There were hurried embraces and farewells, a hasty stowing away of bags, bundles, and passengers large and small in the inside, and of more bulky baggage in the boot.

The inside of the coach was so crowded with Keiths that Stuart gave Ru permission to ride on the seat with the driver.

Aunt Wealthy handed in Wannago's bag and then exclaimed, "Wait! Oh, wait!" and rushed past the well-wishers and the young pastor and his wife into her home. She returned with an embroidered pillow from the settee in her library.

"I never travel without this," she said, hugging the pillow close. "Mother filled it with her own feathers!"

"Was great-grandmother a bird?" Fan asked, looking puzzled.

"No," Adah said. "The feathers came from her geese, silly."

The steps were replaced, the coach door slammed, the guard's horn tooted a warning to traffic on the street, the coachman's whip cracked, and they were off. Millie watched through the back window, until they had turned the corner and she couldn't see her friends anymore. *Jesus*, she prayed silently, *it's more than I can bear. Will I ever see them again?* The familiar town scenes outside the coach window slowly changed to countryside, then long low hills. When Millie could no longer recognize the hills and trees of Lansdale, she laid her head on her arms and tried not to weep.

The few hours' drive it took for the travelers to reach the town where they were to exchange the stage for a canal boat were quite enough to convince Millie that she did not enjoy adventures. The coach was stuffy and became stuffier as the day grew warm.

The rocking stage soon lulled baby Annis to sleep, but the other children had a hard time keeping still. Wannago wiggled and squirmed until Aunt Wealthy was forced to let him out. He settled himself on Don's lap and gazed out the window.

Marcia produced a catalogue and after reading several stories aloud, used scissors from her basket to clip out figures that Adah and Zillah and Fan made into paper dolls.

When the coachman finally opened the door, the young Keiths practically exploded down the step, Cyril and Don tumbling over one another.

"Is this Pleasant Plains?" Fan asked, looking wide-eyed at the new town.

"No," Stuart laughed. "This is where we get aboard the canal boat. But I think we should stretch our legs and have some dinner first."

Stuart let the young ones run until they had used up some of their energy, then sat the family down to a good meal at a hotel nearby. After they had dined, they boarded the packet *Pauline*, which was docked at the wharf. Millie was fascinated by the little boat. It was really nothing more than a floating box; one cabin that housed all of the passengers below, and the deck, which was simply the roof of the cabin. The passengers seated themselves on a cushioned bench that ran around the inside of the cabin, while the hands stowed baggage on the deck. The quarters were only a little less confined than those of the stage. The *Pauline's* interior was so narrow that when the table was to be set for a meal, most of the passengers had to go on deck to be out of the way.

The Journey Begins

When all of the passengers and luggage were aboard, a two-mule team was hitched to the front of the packet. With a shout from the mule driver, the mules started plodding along the towpath. The ropes grew taut, and the packet started to move slowly up the canal. The mules were changed every fifteen or twenty miles, day or night, and a fresh driver and team pulled the packet on.

New passengers arrived at almost every dock and old ones departed, so there was a constant panorama of humanity. When the *Pauline* came to a lock, some of the passengers would get off and walk along the towpath, catching the boat again past the lock. The young Keiths took several such walks with Aunt Wealthy and Wannago as the afternoon wore on.

Finally, the captain announced that it was time to prepare for supper. The passengers climbed the short steps up to the deck. The Ohio countryside, hills green with early summer, dragged by at a slow mule's pace. The passengers found seats on their chests and crates, and children ran amongst them playing tag and making new friends.

Millie sat between Aunt Wealthy and a very large, nervous young woman who introduced herself as Ann Leah.

"I do hope there are no bridges," Ann Leah said, her fingers fluttering to her throat. "I shouldn't want to spoil my dress lying on the deck."

Pappa had explained that when they came to a bridge, anyone on deck would have to get down on their hands and knees, or be swept off the deck into the murky waters of the canal.

"Now, dear, I'm sure the captain would not have sent us all up here if there were any bridges looming," Aunt Wealthy said, scratching Wannago's ears.

Millie's Unsettled Season

Ann Leah still craned her neck, watching the front of the boat fearfully until they were summoned below.

Supper was a simple meal of cold meat and bread. Afterwards the passengers were sent aloft again as the cabin was prepared for the night. The bench they had been sitting on all day was used as a lower bunk, and other shelves hung above it. Blankets were produced, and the passengers settled into their narrow, uncomfortable berths.

Millie helped her mother put the children to bed, all in a group along one wall. Rupert and Fan had the uppermost berth, though Ru had to be careful not to bump his head when he sat up. Adah and Zillah were below him, and then Cyril and Don, left together only when they promised not to talk and to go right to sleep.

Stuart said prayers with each of the children, listened as they whispered their Bible verses in his ear, then went up on deck, leaving Aunt Wealthy, Marcia, and Millie to tuck them in.

"The blankets are all damp," Zillah said. "I don't like it."

"That's because we are on the water," Marcia said. "But they will keep you perfectly warm."

The passengers around them settled into place with complaints and groans. Some were soon fast asleep, while others talked quietly.

"Tell me a story, Millie," Adah said.

"Not tonight," Millie said. "It would disturb the others." She rubbed the little girl's back, feeling her muscles relax into sleep.

Suddenly a rumbling growl filled the cabin. Adah jerked upright. The rumble came again, more terrible than before.

"I heard a bear, Mamma," she said. "I'm afraid!"

"No, dearest. That is just a gentleman snoring." The snorer grunted suddenly, as if he had received an elbow in the ribs. His growls subsided into gargles and whistles, and Adah lay back down.

"I don't like sleeping with all these people," Zillah said. "I want my own bed. I want my own room!"

"Shhhh," Marcia said. "My children must be considerate of others."

Babies cried; older children fretted; some grown people indulged in loud complaints. Ann Leah was much too large to fit on the narrow bench-beds, and so had to spend the night sitting up. All together the cabin was a scene of confusion, and the young Keiths felt very forlorn.

But mother, aunt, and older sister were very patient. They soothed, comforted, and at length succeeded in getting them all to sleep.

Ann Leah, saying that she couldn't possibly sleep, and probably wouldn't sleep all night, offered to watch over the children if Wealthy, Millie, and Marcia wanted to go up on deck for an hour to enjoy the moonlight. Grateful for the offer, the three climbed up the short flight of steps that led from the stern to the deck. Stuart found them seats on some of their own trunks.

There were a number of other passengers sitting about or pacing to and fro. Among the former was a portly gentleman who sat on a crate at the stern end of the boat, his elbow on his knee and his bearded chin in his hand, gazing idly over the moonlit landscape.

After a pleasant half hour, Stuart and Marcia excused themselves, saying that they would watch over the children, leaving Millie, Wannago, and Wealthy on the deck. The *Pauline* glided onward with easy, pleasant motion. All had grown quiet in the cabin below, and the song of the bull-frogs, the dull thud of the mule's hoofs, and the gentle lap of the water against the sides of the boat, were the only sounds that broke the stillness.

"So how do you like travel?" Aunt Wealthy asked. "Is it as exciting as you expected?"

"I don't like it at all so far," Millie confessed. "It is cramped and uncomfortable, and I don't know how the children are going to stand days of this. I thought it would be more... well, exciting."

"But it is exciting!" exclaimed Aunt Wealthy. "The breeze is so refreshing, the moonlight so beautiful."

"Yes, the moonlight is enchanting," said Millie, "and one gets a good view of it here."

"Low bridge!" sang out the steersman suddenly.

"Low bridge, everybody down!" The cry was repeated in louder, more emphatic tones.

Millie dropped to her hands and knees beside Aunt Wealthy, and looked towards the helmsman. The boat was already sweeping under the bridge. She glanced around. The passengers were all hugging the deck, ladies in fine dresses, and dock workers alike—all but one. The gentleman seated on the back of the ship was a lone silhouette against the sky.

"Get down," someone called, but the thinker didn't move. "Get down, I say!"

Suddenly there was a rustling of skirts beside her, as Aunt Wealthy stood up. And then Wealthy was racing down the deck just ahead of the advancing bridge, Wannago at her heels. Millie saw her leap over a small chest, petticoats flying. Then the shadow of the bridge swallowed them, and Millie saw no more.

CHAPTER

6

A Hard Lesson

You shall not covet . . . anything that belongs to your neighbor.

EXODUS 20:17

$\mathcal{M}$illie heard the thud of something heavy hitting the deck, a muffled exclamation, and then silence. The air beneath the bridge was chill and damp with a mist that was rising from the water. It was as if they had stepped though a veil into colder, darker night.

Then the bridge was past, and the moonlight revealed Wealthy Stanhope, sprawled atop the portly gentleman, while Wannago sat — head quizzically cocked to one side — on the box the gentleman had previously occupied.

"I say!" the gentleman freed himself as quickly as possible and helped Wealthy to her feet. "I believe you've saved my life! I was completely absorbed in my thoughts. Can't swim a lick, and I'm sure to have been knocked unconscious by the bridge! I say, Madam! You could have been killed yourself!"

"Nonsense," said Wealthy, straightening her hair and brushing off her skirt. "I am a strong swimmer. I'm sure I would have been fine. A Christian lady does not stand idly by while others are in peril, sir. She does what Jesus would do."

"Incredible," the gentleman said, removing his spectacles and polishing them. "You have just saved the life of Percival Fox, M.D. I am completely at your service, and that of your family." He bowed.

Dr. Fox insisted on helping Wealthy down the steps. It was with some difficulty that she persuaded him to allow her to cross the cabin alone, pleading that his deep voice might wake the children. Wealthy hurried to Marcia and Stuart.

"Who was that gentleman?" Marcia asked.

"A Dr. Hound," Wealthy said.

"I think it may have been Fox," Millie whispered.

"Yes," Wealthy said, "yes, that's right, Dr. Fox." She explained what had happened on the deck in hurried whispers. In the dim light, Millie could just see her mother's hand cover her mouth, and she knew she was trying not to laugh out loud.

"Really, Marcia, it isn't the least bit funny," said Wealthy.

The next day, when they awoke and the passengers went on the deck as the crew prepared for breakfast, Aunt Wealthy looked around quickly. Millie tugged her sleeve and pointed. Dr. Fox was sitting on the same crate that had almost been his downfall the night before.

"Hmmm," Aunt Wealthy said. "This way, children!" She led them to the bow of the ship—and away from Dr. Fox.

It was a beautiful morning, the air sweet with the smell of honeysuckle. Bees buzzed past the packet, and the birds were creating a riotously joyful noise in the tree tops. The passengers who had been most vociferous about their discomfort the night before, greeted one another almost jovially, the light of the sun seeming to make all the difference in their personalities. *Am I like that, Jesus?* Millie had never thought of it before. Her own Mamma and Pappa and Aunt Wealthy had seemed just as pleasant and polite in the damp crowded dark of the night as they were in the cheerful light of day. It was as if what was inside them could not be changed by the world outside of them. *I want to be like them, Jesus,* Millie prayed. *I want to be constant in Your ways and in Your love.*

"Hey, lookit that!" Cyril exclaimed. The mule team had been changed during the night, and a boy no older than Ru

was driving the team. His baggy pants, which were held up by suspenders over his bare shoulders, ended just below his knees. The boots on his feet looked two sizes too big, and his skinny bare legs were spattered with mud. But the most striking of all was the skunk-skin cap perched jauntily on his head, its long tail hanging down his back.

"Pardon me," a deep voice said.

They turned to find Dr. Fox standing behind them. His hair was parted neatly down the middle and curled on each side of his forehead, and he was holding a freshly picked bouquet of wild flowers. He lifted his hat and started a bow, then froze in place, hat suspended over his head, flowers held before him—a chivalrous, but comical, statue.

"Good morning," Aunt Wealthy said, waving away a bee that strayed too close to the flowers. Dr. Fox didn't move.

"Are you quite all right?" Wealthy asked.

The gentleman's lips moved.

"I said, 'are you quite all right?'" Wealthy spoke more loudly.

Dr. Fox blinked twice and his lips moved again. Ru leaned in close, and then nodded.

"He's deathly allergic to bee stings," he explained.

"Well, that's simply solved." Wealthy snatched the flowers from his hands and tossed them overboard. "There!"

"I believe you have saved me again," the gentleman declared. "But you've lost your bouquet…"

"Oh, was that for me?" Wealthy asked. Adah and Zillah giggled.

"Well, er, yes," the doctor stuttered. "I gathered them myself along the path this morning. They were lovely, and smelled so good."

"Bee bush always does," Wealthy said. "You don't travel much, do you, doctor?"

"No, my health is delicate—"

"I thought that might be the case," Wealthy said. "Good day!"

At the first available lock, Aunt Wealthy volunteered to take the children for a walk along the towpath. The steersman was describing the workings of the lock to Ru, but the little ones were all eager to go, and Wannago was beside himself with excitement at the chance to chase squirrels and stick his nose down gopher holes.

Cyril and Don wasted no time at all in seeking out the mule boy, while Aunt Wealthy and the girls spent their time chasing Wannago along the path.

"Now where have they gotten to?" Aunt Wealthy asked, as they returned to the boat. Zillah pointed to the *Pauline*, where Don and Cyril could be seen listening to the steersman with Ru.

When the ladies boarded the packet, Dr. Fox was waiting with a cool drink for Wealthy, a tasty treat for Wannago, and a smile for the little girls.

Millie saw Cyril and Don nudging one another and grinning, and gave them a stern look.

"Would you allow me to find you a comfortable seat?" Dr. Fox asked. Wealthy sighed, looked longingly at the shore, and then accepted.

Millie spent the rest of the morning composing a letter to her friends and addressing it to Camilla. She set it aside to post at the next town. When she went on deck after the noonday meal, the mule team was being changed, and the boy turned to wave at the deck where the Keiths were standing. Cyril waved back.

"Do you know that young man?" Stuart asked, surprised.

"Sure. His name's George," Don said. "He's really nice."

"I wonder what happened to that dreadful hat?" Marcia said.

Cyril flushed. "It wasn't dreadful, Mamma," he said. "It was a real, authentic polecat hide. He got it from a mountain man named Augustus Melodious Malone, who wore it while he fought Indians!"

"I wonder why he would part with such a treasure," Stuart said.

"He sure didn't want to," Don said. "Cyril had to trade him my pocketknife and his slingshot for it. It belongs to both of us now."

"Bring it here at once," said Marcia.

Cyril fetched the hat from beneath the deck, and Marcia examined it closely, checking it inside and out.

"Oh, no," she said, as she examined the inside of the hat. "Did you put this on your head?"

Cyril admitted that they both had, but that they hadn't let Fan touch it.

"That is a mercy, at least," Marcia said. "It is infested with lice." Don's hand went to his head and he started scratching. Cyril smacked it away when he saw Millie looking. Stuart picked the skunk-skin up gingerly by the tail and dropped it over the side of the boat. It hit the water with a plop, and sank instantly out of sight.

"What are we going to do, dear?"

"There's only one thing to do," he said. The boys were made to sit together on a crate until they reached the next town; and then Stuart took them each by the hand and they went to see the barber.

Millie's Unsettled Season

Marcia cried when she saw them coming back, bald as new eggs. The boys had been shaved, and their heads scrubbed and rinsed with turpentine and water.

There was no hiding the smell of the turpentine, or what it meant. Several mothers pulled their children away, and Millie heard them whispering about people with lice. Don and Cyril pretended not to care, but Millie could tell that they were hurt when they overheard several people asking the captain to move them away from the Keiths at the table.

"I can't imagine the impression we will make in Pleasant Plains," Marcia said, putting her head in her hands.

"Now, dear," Stuart said, "It can happen to anyone."

"I am sorry, Marcia," said Aunt Wealthy. "I should have watched them more closely." Dr. Fox, who was hovering behind her, wrung his hands.

"I'm sure you were perfectly vigilant, dear lady," he said.

"Nonsense," Aunt Wealthy said. "I should have watched more closely. Look at them! The poor things are miserable."

Cyril and Don had found seats for themselves behind the steersman. If they stood and walked around the deck, mothers pulled their children out of the way, so the two boys sat close together, ignoring the children who pointed and stared. At every dock, someone new came aboard, saw the boys, shook their heads and moved away.

Finally, Millie couldn't stand watching anymore. "Do you want to play cat's cradle, Cyril?" she asked, pulling a ball of yarn from her pocket. Don looked up hopefully, but Cyril just snorted.

"That's a girls' game. Leave us alone, Millie, or they'll shave your head, too." He put his head down on his arms.

"Itchy head, bugs in bed!" a girl called, scratching her head and laughing. "Bet you're gonna wish you're dead!"

"That's very bad grammar," Millie said, starting toward the girl. How dare she tease that way! Cyril hadn't done anything wrong. He just didn't think about what he was doing.

The little girl ran to the back of the boat where her mother was sitting, and Millie stopped where she was. She turned and almost ran down the steps to the cabin. She rooted through her carpetbag until she found *Ivanhoe*, opened it to the picture of Rebecca, and ran her finger down the tear. *Cyril just didn't think.*

She took the book up onto the deck, and settled into the shade by her brothers.

"Don't yell at us anymore, please, Millie," Don said. "We can't stand it. We're sorry about the picture."

"I wasn't going to yell," Millie said. "I was going to read to you." Soon Adah, Zillah, and Fan were listening too.

Ivanhoe was read and acted out by the young Keiths at the front of the ship. Aunt Wealthy found scarves to be made into ladies' hats, and Stuart made the boys swords from fence pickets he purchased from a lumber barge going the other way. Dr. Fox surprised everyone by offering to read and then doing so brilliantly, almost like an actor on stage. His deep voice was such fun to listen to as it boomed out over the deck, that other youngsters gathered as close as they dared, and looked enviously at the Keiths.

Millie was sitting beside him when he reached the torn page, and she saw the look of disapproval on his face.

"I know, it's terrible," she said, "but Jesus seems to be able to use the book anyway."

"Say what? I don't quite understand. This is not a Bible, young lady. Why would the Lord care about *Ivanhoe*?" He looked so puzzled that she explained the story of the torn page, and how she had struggled to forgive her brother.

Millie's Unsettled Season

"And the most brilliant part," she finished, "is that of course Jesus not only forgave Cyril for tearing His book, He did something wonderful with the book I gave Him. He used it to help Cyril and Don!"

"Hmmmm," Dr. Fox said, polishing his glasses. "Hmmmm." When he started reading again, there was just the tiniest catch in his voice.

Fair Rowena and godly Rebecca were saved, and the Saxon knights defeated and King Richard returned, before the packet docked in Cleveland.

Dr. Fox said his farewells at the wharf, and Millie was surprised to be sorry to see him go. Even Wealthy blushed when he took her hand to say farewell.

"What a beautiful city!" exclaimed Millie as they stepped ashore. "Do let us walk to the hotel, Pappa, if it is not too far."

"Do just as Aunt Wealthy and your mother say," he replied. "I am told it is but a short distance, Marcia. I will have our heavy baggage carried directly to the steamer which leaves this afternoon, and Rupert and the girls can take charge of the satchels and small packages."

"I don't wanna walk," Don said. "Can't we get a hack or take an omnibus? People are looking at us funny."

"Will you walk with me?" Stuart said. "I would be proud for all of the people of Cleveland to know that you are my sons." He took the boys by the hand and the Keiths rallied around them. Wannago and Aunt Wealthy with her purple umbrella brought up the rear.

Millie was thrilled by the sights and sounds of the city. Omnibuses and carriages filled the streets, and pedestrians—elegant in suits, silk top hats, or gowns of pale summer splendor—decorated the sidewalks. Newsboys stood on corners shouting headlines, and a man on the corner offered to shine Stuart's shoes for a penny. The houses were tall and elegant, and Millie wished that Bea could see the gowns and parasols, boots and buckle shoes in the windows of the large, handsome stores. Wannago made the acquaintance of a very fine poodle outside of Roe & Watson, Booksellers. Millie asked her Pappa for two bits to buy a copy of William Lloyd Garrison's paper *The Liberator* at the bookstore. Mr. Martin had brought a copy to school once, and explained that Mr. Garrison was an abolitionist—a person who believed that slaves should be freed. When Millie heard of the horrible conditions of the slaves in the southern states, she decided that she was an abolitionist, too. Millie had never seen a copy of the paper aside from the one her teacher had. The bookseller hesitated to sell her a copy until Pappa intervened, and then he cautioned them about carrying the paper too openly in the street. Abolitionists were considered to be troublemakers, and many people shunned them.

Millie carried the paper folded under her arm until they reached the hotel, and then she read it cover to cover in the privacy of their rooms. There was a wonderful article about Prudence Crandall, a Connecticut woman whose home was burned to the ground because she dared to run a school for Negro children there. There was a very good article about the conditions of the slaves on sugar cane plantations. The writer ended with a plea to give up sugar, as it was a slave product.

"Are you ready for dinner?" Marcia asked, as Millie put down the paper. Stuart led them to the hotel dining room, and Marcia ordered for the children.

"Excuse me," Millie said to the waitress after Marcia ordered lemonade all around. "Is your lemonade sweetened with sugar?"

"Yes, miss," the waitress said.

"I think I would prefer water."

"What's wrong with the lemonade?" Ru asked. Millie explained about the men, women, and children being worked to death on the sugar cane plantations. She had almost finished the story when the tall, cool glasses of lemonade arrived.

Ru pushed his away. "I think I would like water, too," he said.

A man at the next table who had obviously been listening to Millie's impassioned descriptions of the plantations made a loud comment about "slave lovers" as he stood to leave.

Marcia gave him a cool look. "I believe our Millie is right, Pappa," she said. "People should be willing to make sacrifices for what they believe. And I believe slavery is wrong. There are other ways we can sweeten our meals that don't contribute to the misery of others. I'm proud of you, Millie."

No one touched the lemonade, although Stuart said that they should pay for it because they ordered it. When the meal arrived, Don poked dismally at his vegetables. "Are green beans grown on plantations?" he asked hopefully.

"Oh, no sir," the waitress said. "Those are grown in the glorious state of Ohio!"

"Figures," Don said.

After dinner, Stuart, his wife and children went out for another stroll about the city.

When they returned to the hotel, they were surprised by packages addressed to Cyril, Don, and Millie, and a large bouquet with a card for Wealthy.

"'My dear lady,'" Wealthy read aloud, "'Please accept these flowers as a token of my thanks. I am sure I have never met

a family quite like the incredible Keiths. It was a pleasure traveling with you all.' Signed, Percival Fox, M.D."

"Can we open the boxes, Mamma?" the boys asked. "Can we?"

Marcia looked at Stuart.

He nodded.

Paper and string flew, and Don and Cyril pulled out two brand new coonskin caps.

"Pappa! Can we keep them?"

"Of course," Stuart smiled. "You will be the envy of Pleasant Plains!"

"What have you got, Millie?" Ru asked.

"A book," Millie said. "*The Last of the Mohicans*, by James Fennimore Cooper, and a letter."

My dear Miss Keith,

I hope you and your family will enjoy reading this book together—and I wanted you to know how much your story and your copy of Ivanhoe—I mean, of course, Jesus' copy of Ivanhoe—have meant to me. You see, when your glorious aunt saved my life, I was lost in thought about what I had done with my life, and what I should do with my future. I had a successful practice, and all of the money a single gentleman could want. I had respect and honor from my friends, but something was missing. I think I have found out what it was. I, too, have given my future to Jesus. If He can do so much with a tattered book, what do you suppose He might do with a portly, allergy-prone doctor?

When Millie looked up from reading the letter, there were tears in Aunt Wealthy's eyes. "I just love adventures," Wealthy said.

CHAPTER

7

A Dark Day

*A wise son brings joy to his father,
but a foolish son grief
to his mother.*

PROVERBS 10:1

A Dark Day

*T*here were three vessels in port that could take them on the next leg of their journey— a steamboat and two sloops. Stuart let Millie and Rupert decide which they would book passage on. They walked to the docks and looked over their choices. Millie was taken at once by the tall sailing ships. They looked elegant and almost poetic, their masts and lines stark against the blue sky.

"Look at that wheel," Rupert said, pointing to the steamboat. "I'd love to see the boiler rooms fired up!" The steamer was large, and would have more room to carry more passengers, but Millie's eyes kept going back to the larger of the sloops, the *Queen Charlotte*.

Although she (Pappa had explained that boats and ships are always called "she") sat at anchor with her one tall mast bare, Millie could imagine her skipping across the waves, her crisp, white sails fat with wind.

"How about the sloop, Ru?" Millie said.

"She's nice," Ru said without looking at her once. "I wonder what that wheel weighs? Can we really choose her, Pappa?"

Stuart glanced at Millie and winked.

"Of course. But I have been wondering…"

"Wondering what?" Ru looked up.

"Oh, just wondering what it would have been like to sail with John Paul Jones," Stuart said, "in one of the very first ships of the American Navy!"

Stuart had Ru's attention now.

"I thought John Paul Jones's ship was a clipper called the *Ranger*," Ru said.

"Before the *Ranger* was built, Jones was the captain of a sloop, the *Providence*, very much like the *Charlotte* there. She carried 12 guns."

"12 cannon?" Ru was looking at the sloop now.

Stuart nodded.

"And Jones fought more than three dozen sea battles in her, many against larger, better-armed ships. He captured over forty vessels, and sent thirteen more to the bottom of the sea!"

The sloop had Ru's full attention now.

"Captured forty! She must have been fast!"

Stuart nodded.

"I think I would like to sail on her," Ru said, still staring at the *Charlotte*.

Stuart winked at Millie again before he made the arrangements for their trunks to be moved aboard. Once it was settled, it took very little time to stow their belongings.

Millie helped her mother and aunt arrange their belongings below deck, while Wannago inspected their work from a post on Wealthy's berth. The cabins were small, but tidy and private, and Millie felt that she might sleep again at last. No one was more delighted, it seemed, than Wannago, who believed himself to be the instant friend of the ship's cat, Mr. Whiskers. Whiskers, an elegant gray puss with white boots and a snowy bib, did not agree. He leapt to Millie's shoulder and glared down at Wannago with fire in his green eyes. Millie had to usher Wannago from her cabin and shut the door before she could untangle the cat from her bonnet strings.

With the door shut, the cabin was just large enough to turn around in. Millie deposited the cat and bonnet on the berth. There was a small bedside table, a closet just large enough to hang a few outfits, and a small round window. It was a perfect dollhouse room. Millie closed her eyes and spread her arms wide. It was the first time in weeks she had been really, truly alone, with walls and doors between her and any other human soul; it was blissful. She stood for a moment, just enjoying the aloneness, before she hung her travel dresses in the closet. Last of all she set her Bible on the bedside table and smiled. Now it was home.

When everything was in good order, Millie hurried on deck again where Rupert had been left in charge of the younger children. She found him in earnest conversation with a boy not much older than herself. His brown hair was pulled back in a club, sailor-fashion, and held together by tar, like the hair of other sailors on the ship.

"Why do you have that awful stuff in your hair?" Zillah asked.

"Zillah, don't be rude," Millie reprimanded.

"It's a good question," the boy said. "And I don't mind answering. While we are aboard ship there is no time to have our hair cut. This keeps the hair out of our faces while we work. And," he leaned down close to the little girl, "if we should have to fire the cannon, I would use little bits of tar to plug my ears. That way the cannon's roar won't make me deaf." He pretended to clean out his ear with his little finger. "If pirates attack and we have to roll out our cannon, I'll loan you some."

Zillah looked at him doubtfully, and edged closer to Millie.

"Now you are frightening her," Millie said, taking the little girl's hand. "There are no pirates on Lake Erie these days," she said reassuringly.

"That's true enough," the young sailor laughed. "I didn't mean to offend."

"My sister, Miss Millie Keith, Mr. Edward Wells," Ru said formally.

"Edward is the Captain's son," Adah said, a little in awe.

"Happy to make your acquaintance," said the boy gallantly, lifting his cap and bowing low. "Hope you'll enjoy your voyage on the *Queen Charlotte*. We shall do all we can to make the trip pleasant for you and your brothers and sisters."

"Thank you, sir."

"Oh, I hope you will call me Edward," he said, his gray eyes crinkled at the corners. "Your family already does. They remind me of my own young sisters back home in London town. Are you ready to set sail?"

"I don't see how we can," Millie said. "There is no breeze. And the sails are still furled."

"Ah-ha! You would make a good sailor," Edward laughed, taking Millie's arm and pulling her aside just as a yellow blur that must have been Mr. Whiskers went by, followed by Wannago. "But look." He pointed to the steamer that lay along the port side. Sailors were lashing the ships together with fat hemp ropes. "We don't want to miss the tide, so the steamboat will give us a lift until we reach the lake. There is almost always wind enough there to fill our sails. The steamer will give the old *Milwaukee*, the sloop on the other side, a lift too."

"I'd still like to see her boilers," Ru said wistfully, "as she hauls us all."

"She won't even complain," Edward said. "She's that powerful. But when we catch the wind—ah, then the *Charlotte* will outdistance her."

 78

A Dark Day

Millie stood for a moment watching the frantic activity aboard all three ships. Sailors swarmed like ants, carrying loads and tying lines.

"I'm glad we chose the *Charlotte*," Millie said. "She is the most beautiful ship. I can't wait to see her sails unfurled and full of wind. It will be just like the pictures in my books. But don't you think *Queen Charlotte* is an odd name for an American ship?"

"Yes," Edward said, turning quickly away. "Yes, it is odd. Why don't we go aft? The steamer's wheel is about to start turning if I am not mistaken."

Rupert caught Millie's arm and pulled her back as the little ones followed their new friend. "Be a little circumspect, Millie," Rupert said. "Edward is English, after all. The *Charlotte* is quite old you know—older than dear Aunt Wealthy in fact. This sloop was captured—taken from the British during the Revolutionary War. Edward seems a little tense about it still, so try not to tweak him."

"The War for Independence was fifty years ago!" Millie said. "It's ancient history, before our parents were born. How can it trouble him now?"

Rupert shrugged.

"Well, I won't twit him, unless he says something mean or exasperating about Washington or America," Millie said.

"If he does, then twit him as hard as you like, and I'll lend a hand," Ru said. "But he doesn't seem the type. His head is stuffed full of history books, ships, and sea battles."

"Our heads are stuffed full of history books, too," Millie pointed out.

"True. But his books were written by Brits. Who knows what they say about the war." They caught up with their company at the stern of the ship.

Millie's Unsettled Season

The steamer's wheel began to turn, the ropes creaked, timbers groaned, and the three ships started to move. The Keiths watched in fascination as the *Queen Charlotte* and her consorts slowly cleared the harbor.

"That part of the show is over," Edward said. "Come on, let's find some seats in the shade." He led them to a spot sheltered by the forecastle, and they seated themselves on giant coils of rope.

"Aren't you needed to sail the ship?" Zillah asked.

Edward laughed. "I would be, if the ship were sailing. But since she is being towed, there's not much for me to do. When we hoist sail, I'll be needed up there." He pointed to the ropes attached to the mast and jib.

"What's that?" Don asked, pointing to a platform three quarters of the way up the mast.

"That's the crow's nest," Edward said.

"I want to see a crow," Fan said.

"You're looking at one, matey." Edward tucked his fingers into his armpits, and flapping his elbows said, "Caw!"

"You mean you get to climb up there?" Cyril said.

"Not only do I get to, I have to. I keep watch from the crow's nest. I can see other ships, or storms on the horizon, long before the people down below could see them."

"Pirate ships?" Zillah asked, obviously still worried.

"Well, not recently," Edward admitted. "But you never know."

Millie frowned.

"It's really rather boring most of the time. I often carry a book up with me. Father doesn't mind, so long as I don't drop it on anyone's head."

The travelers now had a good view of the Canadian and Michigan shores. Millie thought it was strange to see two countries at once, and how much stranger still it must be for neighbors who lived on opposite sides of the border where the countries were not divided by a river, or any real boundary at all. If, by chance, your pappa owned land on one side, you were an American; on the other, a Canadian. She wondered if God saw the invisible lines between countries that separated families, neighbors, and friends; and if angels were flying over them right now, did they know when they passed from one country to another?

When they had passed through the Detroit River and so far out into Lake St. Clair that little could be seen but water and sky, Edward offered to show them over the vessel. They started with the Captain's quarters and the galley, a tiny kitchen where the food was cooked. They had already seen the comfortable passengers' cabins. Edward gave them the grand tour, leading them down companionways and through hatches, showing them the crew's quarters, which were even more cramped than the berths on the *Pauline* had been, and ending up in the dark hold where the cargo was stored.

"We're underwater here," he said.

Millie touched the wooden wall imagining the deep water beyond. "It's nice knowing the Captain's son," she whispered to Ru. "I can't imagine we'd get the grand tour otherwise."

"Is there anything below us?" Ru asked, stomping on the floor.

"The bilge, full of water," Edward said.

"I expect it's full of rats, too," Ru said.

"Maybe a few," Edward said. "They do climb up the ropes when we are docked. But it's Mr. Whiskers' job to see them off, though he seems a bit preoccupied at the moment."

"I want to go up," Fan said.

"And a very good idea, too," Edward agreed. "It's time for dinner."

Millie was seated at the Captain's table between Rupert and Edward. There were many more passengers of both sexes, several nationalities, and a variety of ages, from infants in arms to hoary-headed grandparents. Cyril and Don had already made friends with a cheerful, mischievous boy named Billy Kress who invited them to sit with him and his mother.

The company was polite and genial, the food was excellent, and every one present seemed content and in good humor. The elder Mr. Wells enjoyed children, and laughed a good deal, making the meal more pleasant still.

"Look," Aunt Wealthy whispered, motioning to the table. "Don't you think that's what the feast of the Lamb will look like? All sorts of people mixed together, laughing and having fun?"

Millie smiled. It was possible Aunt Wealthy hadn't seen Billy Kress slip a bone into his napkin and onto his lap. From there it made its way to Don, who managed to toss it to Wannago, who was hiding under Fan's chair. Wannago collapsed in a happy heap and chewed on it for the rest of the meal.

Millie awoke in the gray of the morning and crept quietly out of her berth. She slipped into her clothes, picked up her Bible, and made her way up to the deck.

"Good morning, Jesus," she whispered. "Thank You for letting me come on this trip. Maybe I do like adventures after all."

A Dark Day

She leaned against the bulwark and watched as the sun came up like a fiery ball out of the lake. There was still no breath of wind. She had a few precious moments to read. She had been in the habit of reading her Bible at least once a day since she had become a Christian two years before. Pappa had knelt with her when she prayed to accept Jesus as her Lord, and then he had given her his own Bible. It had been worn then, but it was positively tattered now. Millie had carried the book with her not only to church and to school, but up trees and under hedges—all of her favorite reading places. Now, it showed the wear and tear of this trip, too, but Millie didn't care. She was so absorbed in her reading that she hardly noticed when the passengers began coming on deck, calling hello and good morning back and forth between the ships. Marcia appeared with little Annis wrapped in a blanket and the other children in tow. The baby was fussing and restless.

"She's getting a new tooth," Marcia said.

"Let me hold her," Millie offered, setting her Bible aside and taking her little sister on her lap. "You can sleep a little longer, Mamma. You look so tired."

"Do take your daughter's advice," Edward said, strolling over to the family. "I'll watch over the rest of the children."

Marcia gratefully accepted. The baby had fussed and fretted most of the night, falling asleep just before dawn, then waking with the sun.

The children explored the ship once again with Edward, and then Zillah arranged a game of tag with the mast as base and barrels and coils of rope as safe islands, and so they played through the morning.

It was almost noon, and Annis was fussing again when Millie looked up to see Cyril and Don atop the railing, looking intently at the deck of the steamer. Edward caught Cyril by the suspenders and pulled him back aboard the ship.

"What are you fellows up to?" he asked.

"Billy said he jumped from the *Queen Charlotte* to the steamer and back again," Cyril said excitedly. "I think I could do that. Can I try?"

"No," Edward said, hauling him back aboard. "It's against the Captain's rules."

"I think you might let a fellow try," Cyril grumbled. "I know I could do it."

"No, you couldn't," said Don, peeping over the ship's side. "It's a big, big place."

"Could too," Cyril insisted.

"Could not."

"Let's go below deck for a bit," Millie suggested. "The baby is fussing and needs Mamma."

Edward gave the children into Millie's care, saying he had to check in with his father, and they followed her as she carried the baby on one arm with Fan holding the other hand. They had almost reached the cabins when Millie remembered her Bible.

"I'll get it for you," Cyril said. "Just tell me where you put it."

"Promise to come right back," Millie said.

Cyril nodded. "I promise."

Millie was trying to quiet Annis by rubbing her gums, when she heard the sound of something heavy plunging into the water.

"What was that?" Don asked. "Are they throwing something in?"

At the same instant a startled cry came from the deck of the *Milwaukee*. "Man overboard!"

A Dark Day

"Man overboard!" The fearful cry was taken up and repeated on all sides.

"Oh, no!" Millie cried. "Please, Lord, don't let it be Cyril!" She ran back the way they had come, the children following behind her. Her heart was in her throat when she saw Cyril standing by the rail with her Bible in his hand. Edward appeared and pulled him away again.

"Billy!" Cyril yelled. "Where'd you go?"

"You fellows sit down and don't move," Edward pushed Don and Cyril to the deck, then jumped to the lines and scrambled up the ropes to get a better view.

"Can you see anyone?" Millie called.

Edward shook his head. "They'll lower a boat," he said.

Almost instantly strong arms were pulling a small rowboat for the spot, already left far behind, where the splash of the falling body had been heard. The crews and passengers of the three vessels crowded the decks, following the boat's movements. The boat's crew pulled backward and forward, calling out to the drowning one that help was near.

"I see him!" cried Edward. "His head's above the water, I see his hat. And they see him too, and are pulling toward him with all their might! They're up with him! They have him now!" A wild cheer rose from hundreds of throats on the ships, but Edward dropped to the deck with a groan.

"What's wrong?" Millie hugged the baby to her.

"It was his hat—only his hat. They've given it up and are coming back without him."

"But they can't give up!"

"It's no use, Millie," Edward said. "He's gone down, and there is no finding him. He's… gone."

Every face wore a look of sadness for the few moments of silent waiting as the rowers returned.

Millie's Unsettled Season

They gained the deck of the *Queen Charlotte*, and one of them—a rough, hardy sailor—came forward with tears in his eyes.

"Mrs. Kress," he said, in a choked voice, "we did our best but we couldn't find him." He held out a blue hat.

"No! Not Billy! No! My little one!" she shrieked. The sailor caught her as she tried to leap the rail herself. Then she fell weeping to the deck.

Aunt Wealthy pushed her way through the crowd, knelt by the weeping woman, and put her arms around her. The woman buried her head in Wealthy's shoulder, and allowed herself to be led below.

Millie wiped her face with her hand. She hadn't realized that she was weeping. Captain Wells did not bother to hide his tears as he ordered the sailors back to work. The sad story spread in hushed tones to the passengers who had not been on deck, and grief for the mother and lost child spread over the ship.

"But how did it happen?" Marcia asked.

"He was jumping back and forth from one vessel to another," said the young sailor who had retrieved his hat. "He missed his footing, and fell in between the *Milwaukee* and the steamer. He must have been struck by the wheel, as he never came up."

"Oh, Stuart! It might have been one of ours," sobbed Marcia, pulling Cyril and Don into her arms. "That poor mother. I was so frightened when I heard the cry. I don't know how I got up the cabin steps! I thought…" Tears choked her voice.

Stuart wrapped all three of them in his arms and held them close.

86

A Dark Day

The sad event of the morning had a subduing influence on all the passengers. Parents kept their children below decks or by their sides. It was a very quiet day on board. Even Wannago gave up looking for Mr. Whiskers and lay with his tail between his legs and his nose on his paws.

When the sun dipped into the lake, the passengers said their goodnights. A breeze sprang up in the night while they were sleeping, and the vessels parted company.

CHAPTER

8

A Brief
Adventure

*They told them, "Go,
explore the land."*

JUDGES 18:2

By daylight the breeze had stiffened into a wind, and the waves rose and fell in mighty hills and troughs. A slashing rain was falling, and the gray lake met the gray sky so that no one could tell where one ended and the other began. The ship tossed about on the waves with a motion that turned the landlubbers in both cabins and steerage pale and a little green.

Millie tried to get up for breakfast, but the floor wouldn't stay still. Each time she tried to take a step, it seemed to move again, and she staggered and stumbled until she gave up and crawled back into bed. Everything in the cabin that was not nailed to the floor or walls was moving, sliding back and forth with the rocking of the ship, until it made her nauseous to open her eyes.

"Millie?" Rupert knocked on the door. "Do you want any breakfast?"

"No," Millie groaned. "I don't ever want to see or smell food again!" She pulled the covers up over her head. She had read about seasickness in her books, but it hadn't seemed as horrible as this. She longed for fresh air, but the rain was falling heavily and great waves swept across the deck. Rupert stopped by to offer her some tea, but Millie couldn't swallow it. "Try to keep your mind off it," Rupert said. "Think of something else. Try thinking about—oh, I know—Edward. He must be up in the rigging now, fighting to keep the sails from being destroyed by the storm. Just imagine the ship rocking below him as the mast sways back and forth, back and forth, like a metronome..."

"Uhhhhhh," Millie groaned reaching for her bucket. "Go away, Ru."

91

Millie's Unsettled Season

By the next day the storm had passed, and they were able to open the hatch and let in some fresh air. All the Keiths had suffered from seasickness, but Millie was the last to recover. It was not until towards sunset of the third day that she could leave her berth. Stuart helped her up the cabin stairs to the deck, where Marcia and Aunt Wealthy had prepared a couch for her.

"Now, dear, the fresh air will help," Aunt Wealthy said, as Marcia tucked a blanket around her.

The little Keiths gathered near their sister.

"You look bad, Millie," Zillah said.

"Real bad," said Don. "Kinda blotchy and pale."

"Run and play, children," Marcia said. "And keep a close watch over them, Ru."

"I'll keep them safe, ma'am." Edward Wells had come up behind her. "I have a surprise for them."

"What?" Cyril asked.

"I found Mr. Whiskers this morning."

"He didn't get drowned?" Fan asked, clasping her hands.

"No. We thought he was lost in the storm, washed away by a wave," Edward explained to Millie. "But I found him this morning. Mr. Whiskers had kittens. I think I may need some help naming them all."

The children laughed with delight as he led them away. Marcia's eyes followed them for a moment before they came back to Millie.

"If I didn't know better, I would think that young man was an angel," Aunt Wealthy said, "sent just to watch over the Keiths! Here's some tea, Millie, dear. It will calm your digestion."

By the time Captain Wells came up to offer his congratulations on her recovery, Millie was almost herself again.

"I am very much afraid my children impose upon the good nature of your son," Marcia said.

"Don't let that trouble you, ma'am. Edward is able to take care of himself. Besides, it's quite evident that he enjoys their society as much as they do his," said Captain Wells, taking a seat near Millie's couch. He remained chatting with her and the other ladies until it was time for them to retire to their cabins.

Fair weather and favorable winds made the remaining days of the voyage a pleasure till one bright June morning they entered the Straits of Mackinac and reached the island of the same name. A fort situated on the 150-foot cliff above them watched over the straits. Millie could see huge cannon barrels protruding from the walls.

"We will lay here a day or two," Captains Wells said, "to take on cargo. In the meantime, would anyone like to feel *terra firma* beneath their feet once again?"

Nearly everybody eagerly accepted. The boats put off from the ship, each with a full complement of passengers, and landed just under the white walls of the fortress. The passengers climbed up a long flight of stone steps. At the top, they entered the parade ground, which was paved with stones and clean as a well-swept floor. On one side of the parade ground were the officers' quarters and the barracks of the men. Three great cannons stood by the wall, giant pyramids of cannon balls by each. Millie followed her parents up another flight of stairs, and they walked along the top of the fort wall.

"I can't imagine anyone ever storming this fortress," Aunt Wealthy said, pointing out how the cannons watched over the harbor and the village of Mackinac.

After they had toured the fort, the Keiths visited the town. Stuart bought them moccasins made by Indians and

maple sugar candy. "It's made with sap from maple trees, not sugar from sugar cane," Millie explained when Zillah looked worried.

"Thank you, Lord," Cyril said prayerfully and sincerely as he sucked the hard candy. "I'm glad you had the afore-thought to make sugar trees."

Wannago escaped from Wealthy long enough to charm the butcher into giving him a sausage by lying on his back, legs stiff in the air. Millie and Fan found him just as he was demonstrating his trick, hoping for another treat.

"Now where did he learn that?" Millie laughed.

"I teached him!" Fan said proudly, lying on the ground to demonstrate. The butcher offered her a sausage too, but Millie politely declined as she picked Fan up and dusted her off. They returned to the ship tired but full of content.

Millie was on the deck early the next morning, as usual, but this time she had not managed to slip away. Her sisters and Ru were with her, Cyril and Don being detained by a lecture from Aunt Wealthy regarding the wisdom of keep-ing buttons and other small objects out of their ears.

Cyril bellowed once, and Millie saw the other passen-gers, who had no idea what was happening, glance at one another. The sound wasn't repeated, so she assumed that the button had been successfully retrieved, and turned back to the sunrise.

"How very still it is! Hardly a breath of air stirring," Millie was saying to her father as Edward Wells drew near the little group.

"We are becalmed," said Stuart.

"And very possibly may be detained here for several days," said Edward, greeting them cheerfully. "And we will have a chance to explore the island. That is, if you will allow it?"

"Oh, Pappa, may we? May we?" chorused the children.

"We will see," he said. "Now watch or you'll miss the sight we left our beds so early for."

The matter was discussed at the breakfast table by Stuart, Marcia, and Wealthy, and it was decided that it would be good for the children to go ashore.

They spent the morning exploring the beaches, catching sand crabs and looking for birds' nests along the rocky cliffs. As they were eating the sandwiches and cheese that their mother had ordered for them, Ru pointed out a cave on a hill above them, and it was decided that they would try to find it by hiking inland, then doubling back. Edward and Ru carried Adah and Fan piggy back, while Millie, holding Zillah's hand, led the way. Cyril and Don were in back.

The trees soon closed around the path, hiding the fort from sight and hushing the sounds of the town and harbor. It was so quiet and still that Millie could almost imagine they were the first people to set foot on this part of God's creation. Even Cyril and Don were quiet, in awe of the hush around them.

They climbed a small hill so that they could see over the trees, and Edward got his bearings. Following his lead, they left the well-worn trail and took a smaller, less traveled way. It turned out that his sense of direction was good, because they soon came out on a ledge beneath a rocky outcrop, and the cave opened up before them.

"Someone's been here, perhaps even lived here," Ru said, pointing to the top of the cave. It was blackened by soot.

"No, not lived here," Edward said and pointed to three white crosses scratched into the rock. "I remember the story now. Three American trappers stopped on this island to trade with the Indians. They had been here before, but there was a different tribe this time, a tribe that didn't know them—a tribe that was allied with the French. When the trappers realized their mistake, they ran for their lives. It was too late to make it back to the boat, and they were cut off. They made the cave, and took their ammunition with them. The Indians were armed with bows and knives and couldn't get to them, but they wanted their scalps for the bounty the French army would pay. The trappers held them off for three days before the Indians built a fire at the mouth of the cave. The trapped men couldn't come out, or they would be shot full of arrows, so they stayed in the cave and suffocated in the thick smoke."

"That's horrible," Millie said.

Edward nodded. "There were French missionaries traveling with the French army. When the Indians told the story and traded their scalps for the bounty of knives and beads, the missionaries insisted that a detail of soldiers be sent to bury the bodies, and they scratched the crosses in the wall themselves."

"Why did the Indians do such a bad thing?" Zillah asked, tracing a cross with her finger.

"It was war," Ru said. "They were fighting to keep the settlers from taking over their land. I expect this island belonged to them, in those days."

Millie thought of Black Hawk and the women and children of his band who died trying to return to their land, and shuddered. Surely God had a plan for America. But men had brought evil with them, and found evil here as well.

Suddenly, there was a snapping of twigs, and a doe broke from the bushes fleeing something below. When she saw the children, she spun on her hooves and raced off in a new direction.

Adah shrieked and clutched Millie's skirt.

"Shhhh!" Millie said, though her own heart was in her throat. "Shhhh. It was only a deer."

"I want to go home," Zillah said.

"We can go back to the ship right now," Millie assured her.

"No!" the little girl sobbed. "I don't want the ship. I want my own house in Lansdale. I want my home!"

"I am so sorry," Edward said, looking at Millie over Zillah's head. "I should never have told that story."

"I expect we'll hear worse where we're going," Ru said.

"Ru!" Millie gave him a stern look, and he shrugged and picked up Fan.

"Let's go back," he said, "unless somebody else wants to explore the cave."

Cyril and Don were all for exploring the cave, but they followed the little band back to the *Queen Charlotte*.

Adah reached the ship looking heated, weary, and troubled. "Oh, Mamma," she cried, with tears in her eyes. "We saw a cave where some trappers were hiding from the Indians and got smoked to death. Oh, I'm so afraid of the savages. Do persuade Pappa to take us all back to Ohio again!"

The mother soothed and comforted the frightened child with caresses and assurances of the Lord's help and care, banishing her fears so that she was willing to proceed upon her journey.

However, with the calm continuing, nearly a week passed and many excursions had been made to the island before they could quit its harbor.

At length one day directly after dinner, a favorable wind having sprung up, the good ship weighed anchor and pursued her westward course out of the straits into Lake Michigan. All night and the next day, she flew before the wind. Then, finally, she rode safely at anchor in the harbor of Chicago. This was the port of the *Queen Charlotte*, where her passengers must be landed and her cargo discharged.

"Now, if you ever decide to become a sailor, Millie," Edward joked, as he handed her from the gangway to the dock, "remember the *Queen Charlotte* has first claim on you."

"I don't think there is a fear of that," Millie said, remembering the nights and days of seasickness during the storm. "I think God must have some other plan for me!"

"I might be seeing you again, though," Ru said, clasping Edward's hand.

"If you do, I'll put you to work," Edward assured him. "No more of this passenger business. I'll have you in the rigging, and on the lines. We'll teach you to be a real sailor!"

He gave each of the little ones a piece of maple sugar in the shape of a leaf that he had bought on Mackinac Island. Cyril and Don received a book on tying sailors' knots and a length of rope to practice on. Finally, he shook hands with the boys and Stuart, bowed to the ladies, and went back aboard to help his father. Millie felt as though she'd said good-bye to a dear brother.

"Isn't it strange how quickly you can become close to someone, Mamma?" she asked.

"Not when they have merry, kind hearts," Marcia said.

A Brief Adventure

"I've often wished I could take them all with me," Aunt Wealthy said, "all of my dear friends. But that would make travel a bit difficult, I suppose."

St. Joseph, on the opposite side of the lake, was the next port to which the Keiths were bound. A much smaller vessel carried them across. They had a rough passage, wind and rain compelling them to keep closely housed in a little confined cabin, and were glad to reach the town of St. Joseph. It was a dreary place without grass or trees. The hotel was a large two-story building. The hot summer sun streamed in through windows, dimmed only slightly by a thick layer of dirt on the panes of glass. The boys fought almost the entire three days that the family was detained waiting for their household goods to catch up.

"Can't we leave sooner?" Cyril asked, after being scolded once again for tweaking Don's nose. "We could take the train or the stage."

"We are past the furthest tracks now," Stuart explained. "There is not even a stage road from this point on, no steamers on the river. The only way to get to Pleasant Plains is by keelboat."

Millie used her time wisely, writing to A, B, and C of her adventures on the *Queen Charlotte* and Mackinac Island. Washing was hard on board ship, so Millie and Marcia now spent some hours with a borrowed laundry tub. When the clothes were dry, Millie pulled them from the line and Aunt Wealthy attacked them with a flat iron heated on the wood stove. Millie folded them, making sure each member of the family had at least one clean outfit for their arrival at their new home. It was hard to believe that after all of these days, their journey was almost done.

Finally, the morning arrived when they started on the St. Joseph River, for the last leg of the journey to Pleasant Plains. The sun shone brightly on the rippling, dancing waters of the lake and river, as they went on board the keel-boat *Mary Ann*.

The boatsmen pulled at their oars and the *Mary Ann* moved slowly upriver against the current, more slowly even than the canal packet. They slid past green miles of unbroken forest. Sometimes one or another would point out a finger of smoke in the distance, rising from the forested hills, but whether it was from an Indian village or a settler's home there was no telling. Sometimes they passed a solitary clearing with a lonely log cabin, and sometimes a little village.

Ragged children ran to watch the boat in either case, mouths open in surprise at seeing strange children on the river. The Keiths waved and smiled, and some of the children waved back, calling greetings across the water.

The river flowed swiftly along, clear and sparkling, between banks now low, now high, and green to the water's edge. A few more buildings began to appear, and then a wagon track beside the river. The sun was nearing the western horizon as, at last, the boat was run in close to shore.

"Here we are, folks," one of the boatsmen said. "This here's the town of Pleasant Plains."

CHAPTER

9

Disappointments

Their hearts sank and they turned to each other trembling and said, "What is this that God has done to us?"

GENESIS 42:28

Disappointments

"Oh, let's not stop here, Mamma," Adah said. "I don't like this ugly place. Tell them to keep going to the pretty part."

Millie took her sister's hand. "Now, Adah, there is no other place for the boat to land. I expect we shall have to walk from here." She wanted to say "walk to the pretty part," but something heavy in her heart told her that if this was the best face Pleasant Plains could show to a new arrival, the pretty part might be harder to find than she hoped. A feeling of dread settled over her, but Millie shook it off. Surely the rest of town would be an improvement over the riverfront.

As the keel of the *Mary Ann* grated on the gravelly shore, a tall figure in rough farmer attire came springing down the bank, calling out, "Hello, Stuart! Come at last with wife and children, and all, eh? I'm glad to see ya! Never was more delighted in my life."

"Hello, George," Stuart exclaimed, shaking his hand. "May I present my wife, Marcia Keith? George Ward." Stuart introduced each one of them as he handed them from the boat.

"I declare, I wish the missus and I lived in town," George said, "but we're three miles out on the prairie. I brought my team along, though, and if you'd like to pile into the wagon, all of you, I'll take you home with me."

"There are quite too many of us to crowd into your home, I'm sure, Mr. Ward," Marcia said, smiling. "We would be grateful if you would take us to the best hotel."

"That would be the Union," George said. "It's not just the best hotel, it's the only hotel. Mrs. Prior runs a clean establishment. I thought you might prefer staying in town, so she's expecting you. Here, let me carry you, bub," he said, picking Don up. "The soil's real sandy here and makes heavy walking."

The sand was difficult to walk in, just as the beaches of Mackinac Island had been, only without the pleasant dampness by the water's edge. Millie struggled along until she reached the wagon. The boys scrambled into the wagon's bed, while Stuart and Mr. Ward handed up first Marcia and Wealthy, and then the girls. They seated themselves on bales of hay. Millie took off both of her shoes and poured a handful of sand out of each.

Mr. Ward took the driver's seat, yelled to his mules, and they were off. Millie was glad for her bonnet, as there were no trees shading the wide street, only huge stumps where majestic trees had once stood. The wood from the trees had evidently been milled and turned into the buildings they were passing—rough frame structures, many without paint, the wood already weathered to a dull gray. Wannago was the only one who seemed excited by his new home, running beside the wagon, and barking happily up at Wealthy.

"That's the tanner's," Mr. Ward said proudly as they passed yet another shabby, gray building. "And this here's the bakery. You can get fresh bread most days." The shop windows were bare and unadorned, and even the signs were rough and plain. Millie was dismayed to see that the sand did not end by the river's side, but continued up into the town, piling up here and there against fences and walls. The wagon pulled up in front of a two-story building painted bright white. "Here we are," Mr. Ward said. "The Union!"

Disappointments

Mrs. Prior, a pleasant-faced, middle-aged woman, met them at the door with a welcome nearly as hearty as that of Mr. Ward.

"I'm glad to see you," she said, bustling about to wait upon them. "We've plenty o' room here in town for new folks, and especially ladies o' refinement!"

She showed them into her parlor, the only one the house afforded. The furniture was plain—a rag carpet, green paper blinds, a table with a red and black cover, Windsor chairs, two of them rocking chairs with chintz-covered cushions and the rest straight-backed and hard. On the high wooden mantel shelf were an old-fashioned looking glass, a few shells, and two brass candlesticks as bright as scouring could make them. Not one speck of dust could be seen. The window panes glistened, and the rough boards of the floor were neatly swept.

"What a wonderful place," Marcia sighed.

"Ha! I'm afraid it must seem a poor place to you, ladies," the landlady said, pushing forward a rocking chair for each. "And you're dreadful tired, ain't you, with your long journey. Do sit down and rest yourselves."

"You are very kind, and it looks like heaven after that keelboat!" Marcia answered, as she accepted the offered seat and began untying Annis's bonnet strings.

"I didn't expect to find accommodations half so good in these western wilds," Aunt Wealthy admitted, glancing round the room. "I thought you had no floors to your carpets, nor glass to your panes!"

"Well, some houses here in town still have the hard-packed dirt. And carpenters here don't make the best of work—I think sometimes I could a'most plane a board better myself. But to get the carpets is the rub. We mostly

make 'em ourselves from rags, but they don't last hardly at all. No use puttin' anything fine on the floor here. Soil's sandy, you see, and it wears the carpets right out."

"They say this country's hard on women and mules," put in Mr. Ward, "and I'm afraid it's true."

Millie saw Rupert's brow furrow at the mention of his mother and a mule in the same sentence, but Mrs. Prior cut in before Ru could speak.

"Now don't be frightening them first thing, Mr. Ward," laughed the landlady. "We don't want them gettin' right back on the boat. Take off your things and the children's, ladies, and make yourselves to home. Here, just let me lay 'em in here." She opened an inner door, revealing a bed covered with a patchwork quilt.

"You can have this room if you like, Mrs. Keith; I s'pose you'd prefer a downstairs one with the baby and t'other little ones? There is a trundle bed underneath that'll do for them. And the rest of you can take the two rooms right over these. They're all ready and you can go right up to 'em whenever you like. Is there anything more I can do for you now?"

"No, thank you," Marcia said. "And these rooms will be fine."

"Then I'll just excuse myself," she said, "for I must go and see to the supper." She passed out through another door, leaving it ajar.

"That's the dining room, 'cause I see two big tables set," whispered Cyril peeping in, "and there's not a bit of carpet on the floor."

"Well, darling," Stuart said, putting his arms around his wife, "the Lord has brought us all safely here. I'll go and see to the landing of our goods, and hope they have fared as well. Will you come along, George?"

Disappointments

Marcia kissed her husband and smiled, but Millie thought her mother's shoulders slumped just a little when he left the room.

"May I take the children to see their rooms?" Millie asked.

"Yes, and help them tidy up for the supper table while you're at it," Marcia said.

Millie found bare floors everywhere, of boards none too well-planed either, making walking without shoes a hazard for toes. The beds were covered with homemade quilts, and everything was scrupulously clean. She poured water from a pitcher into a porcelain basin and helped the children wash their faces and hands.

"Stop it, Millie," Don said, when she checked behind his ears. "It's just sand, see!" He rubbed his hands vigorously through his hair, and a shower of sand fell to the floor.

"How did you get sand in your hair? You haven't been rolling on the ground."

"Wind, I guess," he shrugged. "But sand ain't dirt, it don't stick to you. I expect I'll never have to take a bath again, living here."

"I expect you will," Millie said.

"Yes," said Fan. "We can take dust baths like sparrows!"

"Not before supper, you're not," Millie said, catching Cyril and slicking down his cowlick with a little water. Millie inspected the children, then ushered them downstairs.

The gentlemen returned and the guests were summoned to the table by the ringing of a bell on top of the house.

"Mamma, these cups sound funny," Zillah said, tapping the side of a metal cup with a blue and white glaze, "and the plates do too!"

"Delftware might not be elegant, like china, miss," said Mrs. Prior, "but it suits us here. China cups and plates are hard to replace when they break. Now this," she tapped the side of a pitcher with her two-pronged fork, causing it to ring like a cowbell, "you can pack with you wherever you need to go. You could clobber a bobcat with one of these, and it wouldn't more than dent it."

"Why would one want to dent a bobcat?" Aunt Wealthy asked. Every eye at the table turned on Wealthy. Millie wished she had a napkin to hide her smile, and Ru couldn't hold in his laugh, but covered it by pretending to sneeze.

"What?" Aunt Wealthy looked around at them all. "Oh! I see! You meant dent the pitcher!"

Stuart bowed his head, and the children followed suit. "Dear Lord," he prayed, "we thank You for bringing us safely to our journey's end, and ask that You bless this town, and let us be a blessing to it."

"Amen," Mrs. Prior agreed heartily, and the meal began. After supper, Marcia produced her own bag of maple sugar to sweeten the tea. As she explained about the sugar boycott, Mrs. Prior shook her head.

"I don't believe in slave-holding myself," she said. "But I don't believe I could go as far as you folk. Good for you, though there are some folk in this town who won't hold your opine."

"What about the goods, Stuart?" asked Marcia on their return to the parlor.

"I have had them carted directly to the house; that is, I believe the men are at it now."

"The house?" Marcia said, surprised. "We have a house?"

"It was a 'Hobson's choice', my dear, or you would have seen it first."

"When can we see it?"

"Now if you like. It won't be dark yet for an hour. If you ladies will put on your bonnets, I'll take you round."

"Adah and me, too, Pappa?" cried Zillah eagerly.

"I'm goin'," said Cyril. "Me and Fan and Don."

"You couldn't think of going without your eldest son," said Rupert, looking about for his hat.

Marcia turned an inquiring eye upon her husband.

"Is it far?"

"No, it's on the very edge of town, but we are almost on the edge here. Even Fan can easily walk it. Let them come. You, too, Millie," he said, taking Annis from her arms. "I'll carry the baby."

"We'll make quite a procession," Millie said. "Won't the people stare?"

"Who could help but stare at such an attractive family?" Stuart laughed.

"This way!" cried Rupert, stepping back from the doorway with a commanding wave of the hand. "Procession will please move forward. Mr. Keith and wife taking the lead, Miss Stanhope and Miss Keith next in order, Zillah and Adah following close upon their heels, the three inseparables after them, while Marshal Rupert brings up the rear to see that all are in line."

Everybody laughed and promptly fell into line as directed. They passed a few substantial brick homes, but most of the houses were rough-hewn wood or log cabins. Few had yards of any kind, and one had a pig sitting on the porch, enjoying the shade. People did stare from open doors and windows. Millie tried not to stare back, but Cyril and Don, splendid in their coonskin caps, moccasins, and gaping grins, waved and bowed at the onlookers until Stuart put a stop to it. It was not difficult at all to walk from one end of the town to the other. Soon the houses and buildings were farther apart, and they started up a hill.

"Do you see that yellow frame yonder, my dear?" Stuart asked, pointing to a large building on the side of the hill.

"Oh, my," Marcia said.

"I don't see it," Wealthy squinted. "Is it behind that barn?"

"That's not a barn, it's a house," said Stuart. "Our house."

"No, I mean the barn with the gable-end to the street and two doors in it, one above and one below," Wealthy said. "That's the one I'm looking at."

"I'm looking at the same," said Stuart.

"It looks like a warehouse, Pappa," Ru said in dismay.

"Well, it was a warehouse until recently…but it is the only building large enough to accommodate a family of our size." He looked at the building. "It has several rooms inside, and I'm sure we can make something of it."

"A warehouse." Marcia stood for a moment. Millie stood close, and put her arm around her mother's waist. She could feel the tension in Mamma's muscles, but not a sign of it showed on her face.

"It is a poor place to take you to, my dear." Stuart said, "but it was a 'Hobson's choice,' as I said. There really is no other."

Marcia looked at the building for just one moment more, then stood on tiptoe to kiss her husband's cheek.

"Can't you just imagine Joseph saying that to Mary?" She made her voice deep. "'It's a 'Hobson's choice', my dear. This was the only stable available in Bethlehem.' God had a plan for them, Stuart. And he has a plan for us, too."

"We'll soon have our things, everything you need to make it a home," Stuart said, relief obvious in his voice.

"I have everything I need to make it home right here with me," Marcia said, taking his arm. He put his hand over hers and they started on together.

Disappointments

Millie hung back. The feeling of dread she had experienced upon arriving in Pleasant Plains was not only sinking in, it was taking root in her soul. Stables were perfectly all right for Bible stories. It was nice to think about the baby and the sweet-smelling hay at Christmas time. But this wasn't a Bible story. It was real life. She tried to hold her feelings inside, but they boiled up.

"It's horrid!" The words were out of Millie's mouth before she could stop them. "How can Pappa expect our Mamma to live there? It isn't a house at all. It fronts on the street and the door opens right out onto a sand bank."

"There's a big yard at the side and behind," said Zillah.

"Something green in it, too," added Adah.

"Those are weeds!" The blur of tears in Millie's eyes made the weedy yard swim, looking almost like a garden. If she cried hard enough, this horrible thing might look a little like the home they had left with its large garden and endless flower beds. The June roses and the woodbine must be out by now—the air sweet with their delicious perfume—but they and those who had planted and tended them were far away from this desolate spot. How could she write to her friends that she was living in a warehouse?

"Not a tree, a shrub, a flower, or a blade of grass!" Zillah said.

"Never mind, we'll have lots of flowers next year," said Rupert.

The front door was wide open, as the last load of their household goods had just been brought up from the river, so the Keiths walked right in. The men were carrying in the heavy boxes and setting them down upon the floor of the large room.

"Where's the entry hall?" asked Cyril.

"There isn't any," Zillah said. "No cupboards or closets at all. Just bare walls and windows."

"Don't forget the floor and ceilings," Rupert said. "They are important, too."

"And a door on the other side," said Ada, running across the room and opening it.

"Not a mantelpiece to set anything on, nor any chimney at all! How on earth are we going to keep warm in the wintertime?" Millie asked despairingly.

"With a stove, miss. Pipes run up through the floor into the room above," said one of the men, wiping the perspiration from his forehead with the sleeve of his shirt.

Stuart stopped to settle with the men for their work, and the family walked on into the next room. It was as bare as and darker than the first, though somewhat larger. It had only one window, and an outside door, opening directly upon the side street. Behind the two rooms was a small kitchen with a chimney and fireplace, and a small closet under a flight of steep and crooked stairs that led from the kitchen to the story above.

"Look at this!" Don said, dragging something huge and hairy out of the closet. Wannago threw himself on it with a savage growl.

Adah screamed, but Stuart laughed.

"It's a buffalo robe," he said. "I wonder how it got here? It could have been left by a mountain man, or perhaps it once belonged to an Indian."

"Can we keep it?" Cyril asked.

"I don't see why you shouldn't," Stuart said. "The owner seems to have left it for you." After examining the robe and running their fingers through the coarse brown hair, the children climbed the crooked stairs, followed by Aunt Wealthy and Marcia.

Disappointments

The upper floor consisted of two rooms, the first extending over the kitchen and sitting room. There was a door on one side; Wealthy opened it and peered out at the thin air beyond.

"Oh, my, that's quite a first step!" she said, looking at the sheer plunge to the street below. "What an odd place for a door. Do you think they ever planned to put stairs outside? But the sky is so beautiful, it's almost like a doorway to heaven!"

"You might get to heaven more quickly than you would like if you stepped out!" exclaimed Marcia.

On the other side of the room was another door, which opened into a front room of exactly the same size. There was no way to reach it without passing through the first room.

"Not much privacy," Ru said.

"Millie's right," Zillah said. "This isn't a house! How'll we ever live in it? I want my own room!"

Marcia stood in the first upper room, turning from side to side, a look of bewilderment on her face.

Aunt Wealthy, who had pulled the door to heaven shut, saw it and came to the rescue. "Never mind, dear; it will look very different when we have unpacked and arranged your furniture. Do you know that in China they make walls out of paper? With the help of curtains, several rooms can be made out of this, and we'll do nicely."

"No doubt," Marcia answered. "This front room shall be yours."

"No, no! You and Stuart must take this one."

"I'm quite set on having my own way," Marcia said. "It is the best room, and you must take it. Besides, I should be afraid to have the little ones in there with that outside door opening onto nothing."

113

"We'll nail it shut," Wealthy said, "just in case."

"Well, wife, what do you think?" asked Stuart, coming up the stairs.

"I think it will keep the rain off and the children in," Marcia said. "And it's a great deal nicer than a tent. What more could we ask?"

"I think we could ask for a lot more!" Millie said. "It's a great big dirty barn with plaster all over the floor and spattered on the windows too."

"I hope it can be cleaned," her father said, laughing at her rueful face. "Mrs. Prior can probably tell us where to find a woman to help with it."

Stuart and Marcia seemed determined to discuss plans for the arrangement of the inside of the dwelling, so Millie went back downstairs and stepped outside. The scene had not improved. In one direction she saw only a wall of rough weatherboarding with one window in the second story. In the other direction, a heap of sand and a wilderness of weeds. Behind the house was a small stand of willows and a cow shed. Beyond that, a grassy hillside.

"Could You show me the reason for bringing us here, Lord," Millie said out loud, "because I … I'm dumb with despair!"

"Can dumb folks talk?" Cyril asked, coming up behind her. The family was pouring out the door, like ants from a nest.

"We'll cover it with vines," said Aunt Wealthy, seeing Millie's look.

"And I'll clear the yard and sod it," added Rupert, seizing a great mullein stalk and pulling it up by the roots as he spoke. "Won't be nearly as hard as the clearing the early pioneers of Ohio had to do, our grandfathers among them."

Disappointments

"We will be pioneers ourselves," responded Stuart, who had followed them outside. "Almost pioneers! Let's walk down the hill and around the other side." They followed the road past the yellow house and down the hill. Their nearest neighbor on the hillside lived in a shabby, one-and-a-half-story frame house with a blacksmith shop attached. The sign over the door read 'G. Lightcap', but there was no smoke from the stovepipe nor anyone in the yard. The road curved sharply back down the hill to the center of town, and the Keiths made their way back to the Union.

Mrs. Prior joined her guests in the parlor that evening. "Well, how did you like the house?" she asked.

"I am sure we will be able to make ourselves comfortable there," Marcia said.

Mrs. Prior nodded approvingly. "You can get possession right away, I suppose."

"Yes, but there is some cleaning to be done first, and we'll need help."

Mrs. Prior recommended a woman for that without waiting to be asked, and offered to 'send round' at once and see if she could be engaged for the next day. The offer was accepted with thanks and the messenger brought back word that Mrs. Rood would be at the house by six o'clock in the morning.

"But," suggested Aunt Wealthy in dismay, "she'll need hot water, soap, cloths, and scrubbing brushes."

"I'll lend a big iron kettle to heat the water," said the landlady. "A fire can be made in that kitchen fireplace, you know, or outdoors with the brushwood."

"And brushes and soap can be had at the store, I presume," suggested Stuart.

"Yes, and if they ain't open in time, I'll lend mine for her to start on."

"Thank you very much," said Marcia. "But, Stuart, we may as well unpack our own. I can tell you just which box to open."

"You amaze me, Marcia," he said. "Can we be up in time to be on hand at half past five?"

"We can try. Mrs. Prior, where is your market? I have not seen it yet."

"We haven't got *that* civilized yet, ma'am," replied the landlady, laughing and shaking her head.

"No market? How do you manage?"

"There's a butcher shop where we can buy fresh meat once or twice a week—beef, veal, mutton, lamb, just whatever they happen to kill—and we put up our own salt pork, hams, dried beef, and so forth, and keep codfish and mackerel on hand. Most folks have their own chickens, and the country people bring 'em in, too, and butter and eggs and vegetables, though a good many town folks have gardens of their own, and keep a cow for milk and butter."

"Then I think we must have a little brown cow, with big brown eyes," Stuart said, "for my children must have milk."

"We get a cow!" Fan said, clapping her hands in delight.

"But who will milk it for us, Pappa?" Zillah asked.

"We're on the frontier now," Ru said sagely. "I expect folks here have to milk their own cows."

"Oh, and afore I forget," said Mrs. Prior as she produced a packet of mail, "Mr. Ward dropped these off for you. Had 'em under the wagon seat the whole time." Stuart took the mail and everyone waited as he sorted it—two letters for Wealthy from the Dinsmores, her southern relatives; several for Marcia from friends and neighbors in Lansdale; and one envelope for Millie, fat with pages from A, B, and C.

Disappointments

Aunt Wealthy read the family news from the Dinsmores aloud. Everyone at the Roselands Plantation was well, but Horace Dinsmore Jr. was still away at college and had not been heard from in some time.

Millie carried her own letters up to her room and lit the lamp. She crawled into bed and pulled the covers up around her before she opened the envelope.

Dear Millie, Camilla wrote. *How I envy you the marvelous adventures you write about.* Suddenly, the handwriting changed, and Bea's flowery script continued, *Do tell all about Dr. Fox! Is he terribly handsome?? Are Aunt Wealthy and Dr. Fox corresponding?* An ink blot, and then in Camilla's precise blocky letters again, *How I envy you the solitude you must occasionally experience. Bea is driving me absolutely insane. If I hear one more word about the summer dance...* Bea seemed to have wrested the quill from Camilla's fingers once again. *I am getting to stay up late! I convinced Aunt Alicia — my mother's great aunt — to petition Mother, who petitioned Father, who said he would Think About It! I spent hours, simply hours in prayer. And Father said yes! He said yes!* The rest of the page was filled with Bea's plans for the party. She was plotting to dance with Frank Osborne and at least three other boys. She told every detail of her gown, slippers, and hair combs. Camilla had given up and used her own page to continue, filling Millie in on the goings-on at school. Frank had taken first place in the exams and was planning to avoid Bea at the dance.

Annabeth, too quiet to fight with the other two, had added her own special page with a pressed flower and illustrations of her own design along the borders.

The room seemed to fill with their voices as Millie read. She pressed the flower to her face and could just smell the faintest hint of Lansdale, of gardens and summer breezes. "This isn't Pleasant Plains, it's unPleasant Plains," she cried. The tears flowed freely, and Millie buried her head in her pillow and sobbed. "Why, Lord? Why have You brought us to this terrible place? I'm sure I can't bear it. I can't bear it!"

When the tears subsided, Millie picked up her Bible and opened it, intending to read from the book of Psalms, where she often found comfort. The book fell open to the forty-fifth chapter of Isaiah, and as she glanced down, her attention was distinctly drawn to some words on the page. "I will give you the treasures of darkness, riches stored in secret places, so that you may know that I am the Lord, the God of Israel, who summons you by name," read verse 3.

Millie read the words again slowly. They seemed alive somehow, like they were speaking right to her. Millie's heartbeat quickened. *Could this be what Mamma was talking about when she said that sometimes a Scripture just jumps out at her?* Sweet comfort spread through her. *Treasures of darkness? Riches stored in secret places? Why do I suddenly feel such an odd sense of peace?*

Millie studied the page in silence.

Lord, this passage is about someone named Cyrus, but are You trying to tell ME something? Millie waited for a reply, but heard none. Still, she wondered, could God have something special for them in this gloomy place? Could there be treasure she couldn't yet see?

I'm sorry I was so disappointed in our new house, God. I'm sorry I let my words spill out and make the children disappointed, too. Show me what Your plans are, Lord. Help me be strong. Help me trust You.

CHAPTER

10

Visitors

Mary was greatly troubled at his words and wondered what kind of greeting this might be.

LUKE 1:29

Visitors

*T*he next morning, Marcia left the children with Millie and Aunt Wealthy, and met the cleaning woman at what they had begun calling the Big Yellow House. Millie was determined to follow her Mamma's lead and keep a cheerful heart, no matter what happened. As she put A, B, and C's letter in the pocket of her apron, she promised herself that she would not cry, not shed one tear the whole day, no matter what. Had Rebekah cried when she left her family to travel to a distant land and marry Isaac? No. Had Joshua cried when God sent him to take the Promised Land? No. Would Millie Keith shed any more tears for her friends and home? Never! Millie washed her face carefully, and pressed a cool cloth to her still-swollen eyes.

Mrs. Prior served a good breakfast, and after making sure the children were all dressed and the baby clean and changed, the group set out for the house. Women and children came to the windows of their houses to stare, just as they had the night before.

"I hate this," Millie said. "I feel like a carnival parade!"

"Now, dear," Aunt Wealthy said. "They don't have a newspaper or a telegraph. Newcomers in town must be a source of entertainment."

Millie found out how entertaining after she dropped the children at the Big Yellow House and went to the butcher shop for ham and the baker's for bread. The butcher shop door was ajar so it opened quietly, and she found herself standing behind two ladies of the town, and with them was a girl in a red gingham dress, with dark braids and a plain red bonnet. It was the first girl of her own age Millie had seen, and she wanted desperately to say hello, but suddenly felt very shy. She was glad they hadn't seen her, as it gave her a moment to compose herself.

"You won't believe it," the tall thin woman was saying. "My husband helped cart the goods in, so he should know. He said they've got a real store carpet for that front room, and a sofy and chairs covered with horsehair cloth, and white curtains for the windows and pictures for hanging up onto the walls."

A tingle spread over Millie as she realized they were talking about the Keiths.

"In a warehouse?" the other woman snorted. "That's puttin' on airs. At least the Lightcaps is honest about their poverty. No airs for them!"

"And the little girls wears white pantalets—calico ones such as our youngsters wear isn't good enough for them."

"Ahem," the butcher said, standing up behind the counter and motioning towards Millie with his chin.

The thin lady glanced over her shoulder, then flushed red beneath her fan. "I'll be goin' then," she said, brushing past Millie without saying hello. The short woman followed her out, but threw a brief, apologetic smile in Millie's direction as she went, and the girl gave Millie an open, curious stare.

"Now don't mind Mrs. Gilligut and Mrs. Roe," the butcher said. "This town is friendly like, but the ladies don't have much to talk about. You folks have caused quite a stir. I'm sure we are all pleased to have you."

Millie thanked him, gave him Mamma's list, and asked that the meat be delivered, then hurried home. She found her mother with a broom, preparing to lay down a carpet.

"Will you watch the children, Millie?" she asked. "They are playing behind the house. Ru is with them, but I would feel better if you watched over them all."

Visitors

Just behind the house was a grove of saplings. Millie found Rupert bending down the smaller trees and tying their tops together to make a green, leafy house. The buffalo robe was spread inside it, and baby Annis sat happily in the middle.

"What's wrong, Millie?" Ru said, when he saw her face. "You look like a storm cloud."

"I am not wearing calico pantalets, that's what," Millie said, flopping down by the baby. "And I am never going to make friends in this town."

"Huh?"

"Oh, never mind. Where are the children?"

"Gathering flowers for the house," he said. "Cyril's watching over Fan."

Millie could hear the girls in the distance, prattling to each other, and now and then uttering a joyous shout as they came upon some new floral treasure. In a little while they came running back with full hands.

"See, see!" they said. "So many and such pretty ones — blue and white and purple and yellow."

"Here, Millie," Zillah said. "You take these and we'll pick some more for Mamma and Aunt Wealthy. We'll make a big bunch for each of them."

"Mamma hasn't any vases unpacked yet," Millie said. "Let's make garlands for your hair."

"I don't want no dumb flowers on my head," Don said, coming into the leafy house. "Why do girls do that?"

"To make them smell better," Cyril said.

The girls began sorting the flowers with eager interest, little Annis pulling at them too, cooing and chattering.

Suddenly Zillah gave a start and laid a trembling hand on Millie's arm. There was a look of terror in her large blue eyes. Millie turned quickly to see what had caused it.

"Ru," she said, trying to stay calm. "I think we have company." A tall Indian with rifle in hand stood at the edge of their clearing. He had a tomahawk and a large knife in his belt. He wore moccasins and leggings, and he had a blanket about his shoulders; feathers on his head, too, but no paint on his face, and he stared at them curiously. Behind him was a young woman in deerskin dress with a great bark basket slung on her back.

The Indian man said something in a language Millie didn't understand. She shook her head, and he took a step closer.

Ru's face was very white. "If he touches that tomahawk, I'll charge him," he said, picking up a branch, "while you pick up the baby and run home."

The Indian spoke again, in a different language this time, pointing.

"That's not Indian talk," Millie said. "He's speaking French!"

"He must be a Potawatami," Ru said. "They were allies of the French."

"And the French soldiers taught them to scalp people," Zillah cried, clapping both hands on top of her head. The man turned his black eyes on her for a moment, then repeated, "Ne manger pas bon."

"Please speak slowly," Millie said in her best French. "I don't understand."

The man squatted on his heels by the leafy door, and pointed to Annis.

"Ne manger pas bon," he said again.

Millie glanced at Annis. Petals, leaves and stem of a flower were hanging out of her mouth.

"Oh! 'Don't eat good!' Not good to eat!" Millie said, grabbing up the baby and prying the vegetation out of her mouth. "Thank you! Vous remercier!"

The man's hand flashed down, and he grabbed at a fat black beetle.

"Manger bon," he said, holding it out to Zillah. She cowered back against Adah, who clung to her.

"Cat's sake," Cyril said. "He's just being friendly. Here, I'll eat it." He reached for the beetle.

"Don't you dare, Cyril Keith!" Millie cried, but Cyril snatched the beetle from the man's hand and started to pop it in his mouth.

Just before Cyril got the wiggling bug to his lips, the Indian slapped it away.

"Hey!" Cyril said. "That wasn't friendly!"

"Pas bon, pas bon!" The warrior laughed as the beetle escaped into the grass.

"Not good, not good!" Millie translated.

"It was a joke," Ru said in amazement. "Do savages make jokes?"

"I didn't think so," Millie said thoughtfully. "I don't think savages act this way at all." The Indian motioned for his wife, speaking to her in their own language. She brought her basket close, and poured a pile of berries onto the robe.

"Blackberries!" Zillah squealed, forgetting to hold her scalp. "Can we eat them, Millie?"

"Bon manger." He winked. "Bon."

"Yes," Millie said, "I'm sure Mamma wouldn't mind." She looked at the young woman and said, "Vous remercier."

The woman smiled, restored her basket to its place, and the two Indians walked leisurely away.

"Wait!" Millie called after them. "Please come back some time. Come to our house and meet our parents! I know they would like to meet you."

The little girls gazed at each other in astonishment.

"Oh, weren't you frightened?" Zillah said with a mouthful of berries. "I thought he was going to kill us!"

"Why, they were practically friends and relations!" Cyril said, wiping berry juice from his chin. "I wonder if they live around here."

"I hope not," returned Adah with a wise shake of her head. "I'd rather not see 'em even with their berries."

The feast had hardly ended when they saw a gentleman walking along the road beyond the grove. He wore a long black coat and a tall black hat, and his clean but shabby pants were a bit too wide and a bit too short for his tall, lanky frame. He stopped suddenly on seeing them, then turned and came toward them with a hurried stride, his loose clothing flapping in the breeze. When he removed his hat and smiled, his eyebrows went up, giving him the appearance of a pleasantly surprised scarecrow.

"Good morning," he said, and his large Adam's apple bobbed up and down. "You are the Keith children, I believe?"

"Yes, sir," answered Zillah.

"I'm glad to see you here safe at last," he said, shaking hands with them, "and I should like to make the acquaintance of your parents. Are they at home, in the house yonder?"

"Mother is, sir, but I saw Father go away a little while ago."

"Do you think your mother could see me for a moment? My name is Lord."

Don's eyes opened very wide, and he gazed up into the gentleman's face with an expression of mingled curiosity and astonishment.

"But you know Mamma and Pappa already," he said. "Don't you?"

"I am afraid I have been remiss in my visitations," the gentleman stuttered. "But I would like to speak to them now."

Don stared at him slack-jawed.

"Donald, don't be rude," Millie whispered. "Let me show you the way, sir. They're just cleaning the house." She picked up Annis. "If you will follow me, I will announce you."

"Oh, I'll just chat with the children for a bit, while you announce me," Reverend Lord said. Don trotted along beside Millie all the way to the house. Marcia and Aunt Wealthy were busy overseeing the opening of boxes and the unpacking of the household gear.

"Mamma," Don cried breathlessly, before Millie could utter a word, "the Lord's out yonder and he wants to see you! Can he come in? Shall I bring him?"

"Who?" Marcia asked with a bewildered look.

"The Lord! What does the child mean?" asked Aunt Wealthy.

"It's a gentleman, Mamma," Millie said. Suddenly, Marcia smiled.

"Yes, bring him in," she said, and turning to her aunt as Don sped on his errand, "It must be the minister, Aunty. I remember now that Stuart told me his name was Lord. Millie, don't put the baby down. There are tacks and scraps everywhere, and we will need to clean them up before we set her free in here."

Millie's Unsettled Season

"Lord—that's an odd name for a minister, don't you think?" Wealthy said. "I'm sure I won't forget it!"

Millie explained briefly to her mother about the Indians, saying she was sure they were friendly. Marcia agreed, and Aunt Wealthy beamed when she heard that Millie had spoken to them in French; she had no time to elaborate on the story, because at that moment Reverend Lord came in apologizing for his "neglect in not calling sooner" because he had been engaged with his sermon and the matter had completely slipped his mind.

"I think you are blaming yourself undeservedly, sir," Marcia said, giving him her hand with a cordial smile. "We arrived in town only yesterday. Let me introduce you to my aunt, Miss Stanhope."

The two shook hands.

"Pleased to meet you, Mr. Almighty," Wealthy said.

"Lord," the minister corrected, blushing.

"Oh, my, yes, Lord. That's what I meant. Won't you have a seat?" Wealthy waved at a chair.

Reverend Lord, still blushing, fumbled with his hat, and then seated himself not on the offered chair, but on a box next to it, which was completely covered with paper tacks waiting to be used.

"My word!" he sprang to his feet, brushing frantically at the seat of his britches to dislodge the tacks that were imbedded there. He apologized for this impromptu jig, and his mistake, blushing even redder.

"Never mind," Marcia said kindly. "I apologize to you. We are in such disorder!"

Wealthy gathered the scattered tacks from the floor as Marcia offered the chair again. "You will find this a more comfortable seat," she said.

The young man examined the seat carefully, then sat gingerly down.

"I trust you are church-going folk?" he asked.

"Oh, yes," Wealthy said.

"My husband is a Christian man," Marcia said. "And from the very first day of our marriage we have been determined that our household will follow the Lord."

"Excellent," the young minister said, and began telling them about the church he had recently organized.

Annis grew heavy in Millie's arms, and she realized the baby was asleep. She waited politely for a break in the conversation, but Reverend Lord was excited about every detail of his church, and didn't seem to feel the need to breathe between one sentence and the next. Finally, there was a pause long enough for Millie to break in.

"Pardon me, Mamma," she said. "Annis has fallen asleep."

"Asleep?" The young minister looked abashed. "I am afraid I sometimes have that effect on people. I don't mean to be long-winded."

"Nonsense." Marcia had just a touch of a smile on her face. "The baby is tired and much too young to be interested in church."

"May I carry her back to the clearing?" Millie asked. "I want to be on hand for the other children."

"Yes," her mother said. "I will send Don along with food directly."

Millie said good-bye to Reverend Lord, carried the sleeping baby back to Rupert's house of trees and laid her in the shade. Cyril and Fan were riding saplings that Ru had pulled over for them, pretending they were horses, while Zillah and Adah finished their garlands of flowers. Millie cautioned them to be quiet while the baby slept, then leaned back against a nearby tree.

"What kind of a place have You brought us to, Lord?" she asked. "This doesn't seem much like the promised land at all! Public gossips, savages that want to be friends, and I know, Lord, that You call Your ministers, and I know You choose them. But this one," Millie glanced around to make sure no one was listening, and lowered her voice anyway, "this one looks like Ichabod Crane! This place is never, never going to feel like home!"

Home. Suddenly she realized that the same ghost moon that was looking down on her from the bright afternoon sky was looking over Lansdale, too. Bea and Annabeth and Camilla might be gazing up at it right now, wondering about her. She took the letter from her pocket and pressed it against her heart. Could they ever imagine what a strange and horrible place she had come to?

"They wear calico pantalets, Bea," Millie whispered. "And you would hate it, Annabeth. Camilla, I haven't seen a single book since I arrived, and I'm sure they haven't any!"

CHAPTER

11

Home At Last

Enlarge the place of your tent, stretch your tent curtains wide, do not hold back; lengthen your cords, strengthen your stakes.

ISAIAH 54:2

*M*illie's eyes misted with emotion. *I am not going to start that again!* She pulled her knees up and rested her chin on them.

"Trust in the Lord with all your heart and lean not on your own understanding. In all your ways acknowledge him, and he will make your paths straight." Could it have been only months since her mother had given her that verse? That trusty chair in the washroom seemed a hundred years in the past. It hadn't let her fall. *But I feel like I'm falling, God. I feel like I'm tumbling, tumbling down, and I just haven't hit the ground yet.* That was just it. She hadn't hit the ground. Maybe she wasn't falling at all.

Mamma has lost a lot more than I have, and she is still trusting God. Jesus, I want to trust You like that. I want to know You like that. But I don't know how yet. Millie sat up and straightened her shoulders. *I'm going to try to be like Mamma while I learn.*

Suddenly the Scripture from the night in the hotel came back into her mind, sharp and clear: *"I will give you the treasures of darkness, riches stored in secret places, so that you may know that I am the Lord, the God of Israel, who summons you by name."*

"Jesus," Millie prayed, "are You going to show me the treasures hidden in Pleasant Plains?"

Just then, Don came running from the house, carrying a covered basket. All the little Keiths gathered around the door to their leafy playhouse.

"He wasn't the Lord at all," he announced, setting the basket down, "and he didn't talk long. Well, not long for a preacher," he corrected himself. "I guess 'cause he was uncomfortable on account of sitting on a bunch of tacks.

Mr. Hendrix at home never sat on tacks, and he always talked longer. But Mamma sent us a picnic, anyways."

"I'm not too hungry," said Adah. "Did you tell Mamma about the Indians and the berries?"

"Yes, Millie told her most everything already," he glared at Millie, "but I told her about the beetle. And she says we needn't be a single bit afraid; they sound like nice folks. And she said to tell Cyril not to try eatin' any more beetles."

"Well, I'm as hungry as a bear," Ru said. "Let's eat."

"Wait," Millie said. "We need to say a blessing first."

"I'll do it," said Cyril, "That way it'll be quick." He closed his eyes and folded his hands. "Dear Lord, we thank You for the gingerbread and turnovers and—and all good things, like berries, beetles, and snakes."

Millie's eyes flew open, and she looked around quickly, but Cyril's hands were still folded, and his head bowed. He looked almost angelic with the sunlight illuminating the fuzz on his head.

"Amen. Now gimme mine, Millie." He held out both hands.

"What snakes?" Millie asked.

"It got away," Cyril said.

"Snakes don't like pockets, I guess." Don reached for the basket.

Millie glanced at Ru. He just shook his head.

"Ladies first," Millie said, gently pushing Don's hand away. "Now spread your handkerchiefs in your laps to keep the greasy crumbs from your clothes. Adah, Zillah, and Fan may help themselves."

"Go ahead, Millie," Ru said, when the little girls had chosen a sandwich. "You're a lady."

"No, I'll serve myself last, the way Mamma does."

There was more than enough for them all. Millie made sure the remains of the meal were put carefully back in the basket, then hung it up on a branch near at hand. As she did so, Adah squealed, "Mamma's coming!" Annis woke at the commotion and started to cry.

"May I come in?" Mamma asked at the door.

"Yes," Zillah said.

Marcia wiped her feet neatly on the grass, then stooped to enter their little house. She sat down on the robe and took Annis in her arms.

"Did you have enough to eat?" she asked.

"Yes," Ru said. "Thank you, Mamma."

"You quite deserved it, taking care of yourselves and Annis all morning, and not giving any trouble to anybody."

Fan covered her with sticky kisses, and she laughed. She had to hear the story of the Indians all over again, with each one adding a new detail, and Don and Cyril acting out the parts of the Indians, complete with leaves in their hair instead of feathers.

"Are you getting done fast, Mamma?" Zillah asked. "Can we sleep in the Big Yellow House tonight?"

"Not tonight. We've scrubbed the wood floors and I want them to dry thoroughly before we move in. We will go back to the Union for our supper and to sleep tonight. But tomorrow…"

"We will be in our own house!" Fan yelled.

"Not the nice house we used to have, though," sighed Zillah.

"What!" Marcia said. "You are not telling me you don't like our new home! Did Indians ever visit at our old house? Just think of it! They were the first of our new neighbors to greet us! And we had no buffalo robes, or houses made

of saplings to play in. It is not the same, but I am sure God has a very good plan for the Keiths!"

Annis had returned to her nap in her mother's arms. Marcia laid her down gently on the robe and pulled a light covering over her, then motioning them to follow her, she crept from the little house and brushed off her apron. From its pocket she drew out a book of stories for Millie to read to the younger ones.

"Now mind the baby," she said quietly. "I have to go back and help Aunty."

"Read a story, Millie," Cyril said, and then as an after-thought, "Please?"

"I'll read 'Androcles and the Lion'." Millie flipped through the book. "You always like that."

"An' then the one 'bout the girl that had a silk dress and couldn't run and play 'cause her shoes pinched," begged Fan.

"Look!" exclaimed Adah in an undertone. "Those girls haven't got silk dresses or shoes to pinch their toes. Don't they look odd?"

Two little girls—one about Adah's size, the other a trifle smaller—were standing just at the edge of the Keiths' clearing, looking longingly toward the spot where the Keith children were seated.

They had sunburnt faces, and dark braids fell over their shoulders. Their thin little forms were scarcely covered by their faded, worn, calico dresses. Pantalets of the same material but different color, showed below their skirts. Their feet were bare, and very brown, and on their heads were sunbonnets of pasteboard covered with still another pattern of faded calico.

"Can we ask them to come and join us?" queried Zillah. "Please, Millie! They could be company in our house!"

"You may be the hostess," Millie said to her.

"Good afternoon, little girls," said Zillah, though they must have been close to her age. "Will you come and sit with us?"

They shook their heads, and the younger one put her thumb in her mouth. Zillah looked at Millie.

"Perhaps they are shy," Millie whispered. "Let's just start to read and see what happens. Don't stare at them, now." She began the story, glancing up after a few paragraphs. The little strangers had edged closer. Millie lowered her voice, as the story was getting exciting. The next thing she knew, the little girls were sitting on the edge of the robe, just as intent as the other children.

Zillah and Adah were clearly more interested in the newcomers than in the story. When she finished, Millie closed the book and smiled.

"Hello," she said. "My name is Millie Keith. What's yours?"

"Emmaretta Josetta Lightcap," said the bigger girl, "and this is Minerva Louisa Lightcap. She's my sister. We call her Min."

Min nodded without taking her thumb from her mouth.

"My name is Zillah, and this is Adah, and Ru and Don and Cyril and Fan, and our baby Annis is sleeping," Zillah said, and then, remembering that she was the hostess, "May I offer you some tea?" She leaned toward Emmaretta and whispered, "I don't really have any tea. But we have some good things in our basket."

"Thrilled and delighted," said Emmaretta.

Ru handed the basket down from the branch, and Zillah opened it up, spread a napkin for a tablecloth, and set out

the remains of the feast. Emmaretta and Minerva helped themselves. Every time they finished one delicacy, Zillah produced another.

Millie settled back to reading, while the girls concentrated on finishing every crumb left in the basket. They had completed the job when they were summoned by a woman's voice from the direction of the smithy.

"That's our mother," Emmaretta explained.

Min nodded, licked a smear of jelly from her finger, then put her thumb back in her mouth.

"You must come calling," Emmaretta said, wiping her hands on her skirt. "I don't have any tea, either, but Gordon found a bee tree last week, and we've got honeycomb!" Then they turned and ran for home.

Millie helped Marcia and Aunt Wealthy put the finishing touches on the house the next day. By mid-afternoon, everything was in order.

"Ahhhhh," Stuart said, sinking into his chair, when he returned from arranging his office in town. "There is nothing like your own castle!"

"There is no castle, Pappa," Adah said. "Just our house."

"Are the floors clean?" Stuart asked.

"Yes," Zillah said.

"And we all have rooms, and beds?"

"Our walls are made out of curtains," Zillah said.

"Do we have chintz-covered and cushioned lounges, and pretty, dainty tables?"

"They are made of packing crates, Pappa," Adah laughed. "Mamma just covered them with fabric!"

"See?" Stuart said. "A castle. Too bad the moat has filled up with sand. I would like to go for a swim."

"It's time for supper, your majesty," Marcia said, appearing at the door. The family gathered about a neatly appointed table set out in the center of one of the three lower rooms. They all bowed their heads as Stuart prayed, blessing the meal, their new home, and his family.

"We are going to have a new addition to our family," Stuart announced as the meal began. Millie looked at her mother, but she looked just as puzzled as the rest of the gathering at the table.

"Her name is Belle. She has sad eyes, and I expect all of you will be kind to her until she gets used to her new home." He winked at his wife, then said, "Would you pass the bread, Millie?"

"A new girl, Pappa?" Fan said. "Will she sleep in my bed?"

"Oh, no," he said. "I don't expect she would fit in your room. And she might have some trouble with the stairs. I think she'll have to stay in the shed by the willow trees."

"I'll stay there with her then," Fan said, "so she won't be afraid."

"She's not going to be afraid, you goose," Ru said. "Pappa would never make a real girl sleep in the shed. He's bought a cow! Isn't that right, Pappa?"

"A cow!" There was a great deal of excited talk among the children over who would feed it and milk it.

"When will we get her?" Aunt Wealthy asked. "I'll show the children how to milk."

"If there is light after supper, Ru can fetch her. I bought her from Mr. Rinwald, who lives across town. She will sleep in the shed. We will feed her sweet hay and let her

graze in the field on the other side of the hill. I think walking her to the field will be a job for Cyril."

Cyril sat up taller. "Mebbe you can help," he said to Don. "Sometimes, anyway."

Ru left as soon as the meal was finished to get the cow. Aunt Wealthy and Stuart and Marcia sat on the porch enjoying the evening, while Millie and the younger children cleared the table, washed the dishes, and made the kitchen all neat.

"Ru's comin' back!" Don yelled. "He's got the cow!"

The entire family assembled in the yard as Ru walked the little brown cow into the yard.

"She's beautiful!" Millie said, and everyone had to agree. She had a sweet face, and long black lashes over her big brown eyes. The family followed Ru to the cow shed, where he tied her halter to the rail.

"She's full of milk, too," Aunt Wealthy said. She called for a stool and a bucket, and gave the family their first lesson in milking. The little cow looked around quizzically as Aunt Wealthy settled the stool and bucket in place, but soon returned to chewing her cud placidly, as Aunt Wealthy began to milk.

"You grab a teat like this," she said, demonstrating. "Pinch it between your thumb and finger, just so…and squeeze!" A stream of milk shot into the bucket. Wannago watched in fascination until Wealthy directed a stream of warm milk at his face. He jumped back, then licked his chops and sat on his hind legs begging for more. He caught the next stream in his mouth, and everyone laughed.

"You are amazing, Aunty," Marcia said, when Belle's udder was empty and the bucket full. "I didn't know you knew how to milk!"

"Tsk, Marcia," said Wealthy. "You can't live to my ripe age without learning a thing or two!"

Stuart put some fresh hay in the cow's trough, and shut the shed for the night.

This done they returned to the sitting room. The great family Bible lay open on the table before Stuart, a pile of hymn books beside it. Rupert passed out the hymnals while Stuart read a few verses of Scripture, then led them in a hymn. Marcia's sweet voice sang harmony, and the others joined in as a full chorus of praise filled the Big Yellow House.

When it died away, Stuart prayed for each of the children before he sent them up to bed. Each little one came to claim a goodnight kiss from Mamma, Pappa, and Aunt Wealthy, then cheerfully followed Millie up the steep, crooked stairway to the large room above, to sleep and dream their first dreams in the Big Yellow House.

CHAPTER

12

First Impressions

What I feared has come upon me;
what I dreaded has happened
to me.

JOB 3:25

*M*illie awoke the next morning to the feel of her own pillow, the smell of Mamma's lavender soap—and someone shaking her shoulder.

"Wake up, Millie," Fan said. "I want to ride the cow."

"Don't be a goose," Millie said sleepily. "People don't ride cows. Where are Mamma and Pappa?"

"They went to see about Pappa's new office, and they took Ru. And Aunt Wealthy is walking all over town, talking to God. She said to let you sleep, but I want to ride the cow, too!"

Millie was suddenly wide awake. "What do you mean, *too*?"

"Don said he was going to ride it," Fan said. "He said I was too little!"

Millie jumped out of bed and rushed downstairs in her nightgown and bare feet. She made it out the back door just in time to see Don launch himself from the fence onto poor Belle's back. Belle turned her head placidly to look at him, then started to walk.

"Wahooo!" Don yelled. Cyril shouted encouragement from the fence, where he was perched holding one end of a rope he'd tied to Belle's halter. Belle reached the end of the rope, gave one jerk, and the rope came off the halter. Wannago raced ahead of her, yapping happily.

"What kinda knot was that?" Cyril said, jumping off the fence.

"Slip knot, I'd guess," Don said, kicking his heels against Belle's sides.

"Bring her back here, Don! I wanna get on, too!" Cyril yelled. Belle had her own ideas, it seemed, and they had something to do with the wide-open prairie beyond the hill.

"Don! Get off that cow this instant!" Millie called.

"I can't," Don yelled back. "She's too high. I'll bust a leg!"

"Where are you going?" Cyril demanded, starting after them.

"Wherever she wants, I guess," Don replied.

Belle was trotting now, Don bouncing like an India rubber ball on her back.

She changed her mind about the prairie, and turned and started down the street toward the center of town.

"This is not happening!" Millie cried. "What will people say? We will be the family who lives in a warehouse and rides cows!" She picked up her long cotton nightgown and ran, catching Belle by the halter just as they passed the blacksmith's shop.

"Aw, Millie," Don said. "Just when she was goin' good, too!"

"That's a pretty dress."

Millie glanced around quickly. The two little girls from the willow grove were standing in the front yard.

"Real pretty," Emmaretta said. Minerva nodded agreement, thumb firmly in her mouth. Behind them stood an older girl. She smiled, but Millie ducked her head in embarrassment, and pulled on Belle's halter.

"No more riding the cow," she said firmly as she tied Belle up. "Pappa will be very upset when he learns how you have treated her." She made sure the cow had water and alfalfa, then stopped at the well to pull up a bucket of water to wash her dusty feet. The foot washing was a success, but

the hem of her nightgown was all muddy when she was through. She sighed as she went back up the stairs to the kitchen.

"Millie, is that you?" Marcia called.

"Yes," Millie said, stomping into the dining room, "And you won't believe what Don has done now—"

Marcia was standing with a finely dressed woman and two girls about Millie's age. They wore bright, pretty bonnets and carried a basket of freshly baked bread, jars of homemade jam, and just-picked daisies.

Marcia blinked at Millie's muddy nightgown and unbrushed hair, took a deep breath and said, "And this is Mildred, my eldest daughter, the one I was telling you about, Mrs. Chetwood."

Millie self-consciously smoothed her nightgown, torn between the desire to strangle Don and the wish to sink into the floor. Both girls' eyes traveled from Millie's muddy hem to the furniture made of crates and covered with fabric.

Millie had never felt poor before, never in Lansdale, even after Pappa's money was gone, and not even when Pappa had shown them the Big Yellow House. But suddenly she saw the Big Yellow House not as Pappa's pretend castle, but as her home, made of broken parts and pieces and leftover goods.

"Oh, never mind your nightgown, dear girl," Mrs. Chetwood said, sensing her embarrassment. "I know you weren't expecting us—we met your mother at the door. We just wanted to stop by and say 'Welcome to Pleasant Plains.' My, you look so much like your mother! This is my daughter Claudina Chetwood. She's thirteen and her good friend here, Lucilla Grange, is nearly fourteen." Mrs. Chetwood smiled graciously.

Millie's Unsettled Season

The two girls curtsied. Millie returned their gesture. She heard a nervous giggle, and to her horror realized the sound was coming from her own throat.

"I was chasing a cow," she started to explain, but gave up. "Mamma, will you excuse me for a moment?"

"Of course," Marcia said, and Millie practically flew out of the sitting room, through the kitchen and up the stairs. She pulled on her petticoats and skirt, and ran a brush through her hair.

"Give me courage, Lord," she prayed as she started back down the stairs.

"So, my husband and yours will no doubt meet, if not today then very soon," Mrs. Chetwood was saying when Millie entered. Aunt Wealthy had returned from her walk, and was listening attentively as well. "Dr. Chetwood is the local physician and his office is only a few doors down from the one your husband has taken. And Mr. Grange runs the bank, so I'm certain they'll meet, if they haven't already. Mrs. Grange, Lucilla's mother, would have come with us but she is feeling poorly, I'm afraid. Sends her warmest regards."

"I hope it is nothing serious," Aunt Wealthy said to the girl. "Let us know if there is anything at all we can do for her."

"Thank you, ma'am. I will tell her of your concern." Then she turned to Millie. "Do they call you Mildred," she asked, "or do you have a nickname?"

"Most people back in Lansdale called me Millie."

"I hope you will allow us to call you that, also?" Lucilla said properly, and then, smiling, "You can call me Lu."

The ladies said their good-byes, promising future visits. Marcia offered her great thanks for the visitors' courtesy and the lovely basket.

"Not at all, Mrs. Keith. I suspect you would have done the same. So very nice to meet you too, Miss Stanhope. I do hope we all become friends," Mrs. Chetwood said, clasping first Marcia's hand and then Aunt Wealthy's.

Millie thanked the girls for stopping by.

"You must return the visit," Claudina said.

"Yes, you must," Lu said.

"I am never going out in public again," Millie said, smiling through clenched teeth, as she stood at the door waving good-bye. "Never."

"Nonsense," Aunt Wealthy said. "I think you will be great friends with those girls."

Millie watched as they made their way down the street, past the piles of sand and weeds. Then she ran up to her room, threw herself on her bed, and covered her head with a pillow. *Great friends? After the way they looked at me?* She sat up and threw her pillow across the small room. She didn't need any friends. She had her books, and books never judged you because of the clothes you wore, or the house you lived in. But they didn't talk much, either. Millie picked up her pillow, splashed water on her face, and went downstairs to help Mamma and Aunt Wealthy with the day's chores.

⁓

The next few days were a whirlwind of constant activity and hard work for Millie and the whole Keith family. Marcia and Aunt Wealthy had done a great deal of work on the Big Yellow House, but there was still much to be done.

In addition to his new responsibility for Belle, Rupert discovered gardening and carpentry, and Cyril and Don and

Fan were under his feet all day trying to help as he worked on the house, or broke ground for a garden. Millie and the older girls helped Marcia and Aunt Wealthy about the house, or tended to Annis.

Stuart bought a churn, and Aunt Wealthy showed Millie how to skim the cream off the top of the buckets of frothy milk and churn it into butter. When the butter was formed, she poured it out on a slab, mixed salt in, and then formed it into blocks that were stored in the cool well with the milk. All of the young Keiths thought that Belle's butter was the best they had ever tasted.

Even Mrs. Prior agreed, when she stopped by for a visit on Saturday evening.

"Are the neighbors making friendly yet?" she inquired after she had finished her buttered scone.

"Mrs. Chetwood brought her daughter and Lucilla by," Wealthy said. "They seemed very friendly."

"The others will come along, I'm sure," she said. "I expect they are set back by Stuart being a lawyer. Oh, and if you are looking for a girl to help around the house, I hear Celestia Ann Huntsinger is looking for a place. Her pa has a lot of mouths to feed. She's seventeen years old, and a real hard worker. I must be going. Now don't you be formal with me, but run in whenever you can. I'll always be glad to see you."

Stuart stood to walk her home, as it was already dark outside.

"No, never mind your hat, Mr. Keith. I don't want a beau, and I'm not the least mite afraid of walking alone. Goodnight to you all."

The candle flared in the draft from the open door. Aunt Wealthy hastened to snuff it. "These are miserable candles. If you will get me some tallow tomorrow, Stuart, I'll make

a better variety. We have the molds and the wick; all we need is the tallow."

"Cow milking and candle making. You do amaze me, Miss Stanhope!" Stuart said.

"We are lucky to have you," Marcia agreed. "There is so much to do, I would be lost without you, Aunty." Stuart looked thoughtfully from one to the other.

"What do you think, wife?" he asked. "Should we hire the girl Mrs. Prior mentioned?"

"If she is a hard worker, she would be of some help," Marcia said. "And if she needs a place, we could be of some help to her."

"Then it sounds like a match," he agreed. "I'll have Mrs. Prior send her around."

The Keiths were up and dressed early the next morning, for it was the Sabbath. Millie took special care as she chose the little girls' dresses and bonnets, and Stuart inspected each of the boys from head to foot before they set out along the narrow foot path that led past the grove of saplings to the little church.

The tall grass on each side of the trail was still wet with dew, and Millie showed Zillah and Adah how to lift their skirts and jump the puddles so as not to soil their shoes. Cyril kept wandering from the path anyway, following Wannago on his adventures, and his britches were soaked to the knee by the time they reached the church.

Reverend Lord was standing on the steps, greeting each family as they arrived. His Sunday suit was long enough in the arms, and even the pants fit well.

"Good morning," he said, shaking Stuart's hand. "I am glad to meet you at last! I think your family will double my Sunday school enrollment!"

Millie's Unsettled Season

Wealthy spoke firmly to Wannago, and he lay down to wait on the steps.

Most of the families attending were townsfolk who arrived walking like the Keiths, but a few families had come in from the surrounding country in wagons. There was little display of fashion or style in dress. Most of the women and girls wore calico.

Claudina Chetwood and Lucilla Grange smiled at Millie as she entered. The inside of the church was very different from any the Keiths had been in before. The windows were plain glass, and the seats rough wooden benches without a back. There was no organ or even piano.

"This doesn't look like a church at all," Zillah whispered as they took their seats.

"Shhhh," Millie said. "The sermon is about to begin."

The last member having arrived and been duly greeted, the Reverend Lord shut the door and strode up the center aisle. He stood for a moment behind his rough pulpit, and then he asked the people to join him in prayer and bowed his head.

As he spoke, his awkwardness fell away. Millie could almost hear the water lapping at the sides of the boats as he spoke of Jesus in Galilee. People young and old sat transfixed by his words. How could she ever have thought he looked like Ichabod Crane? For the first time in weeks, Millie felt truly at peace.

When the sermon was over, they stood for a hymn.

"Pappa, where are the hymnals?" Zillah whispered. "I can't find one!"

"Just listen," Stuart said.

Reverend Lord began the hymn by calling out the first line of a familiar hymn, then the congregation sang that verse together. Just as they finished, he called out the first

line of the second verse, and so it continued until they had finished the hymn.

People lingered after church, complimenting Reverend Lord on his sermon and text, discussing the happenings of the week. The Keiths were warmly welcomed, and assured of intentions to call. Many people expressed hopes that they would "like the place," the country people adding, "Come out and see us whenever you can."

Millie had almost forgotten her embarrassment of the day before when Claudina Chetwood approached her and smiled, her deep dimples peeking out.

"I'm hosting a young ladies' Bible study at my house on Wednesday," she said. "Would you be interested in coming? Many of the girls from church will be there, and Mother will serve us a light meal."

"I would love to attend," Millie said. "But I'll have to ask Mamma first." They found Marcia just as a tall, gaunt woman approached her.

"Oh, dread," Claudina whispered. "I'll wait for your answer, Millie. I think my mother wants me just now." Millie watched in surprise as the girl walked quickly away.

The woman who had approached Marcia was of uncertain age. She had yellow hair and pale, blue eyes. Her dress was almost austere in its simplicity: a dove-colored calico, cotton gloves of a darker shade, a white muslin handkerchief crossed on her bosom, a close straw bonnet with no trimming but a piece of white ribbon put straight across the top, brought down over the ears and tied under the chin.

"My name is Drybread," she announced with a slight, stiff curtsy. "Damaris Drybread."

"Mrs. or Miss?" queried Marcia pleasantly.

"Miss. And yours?"

"Mrs. Keith. Allow me to introduce my aunt, Miss Stanhope, and my daughter, Mildred. These little people also belong to me."

"Do you go to school, my little lass?" asked the visitor, unbending slightly in the stiffness of her manner as she addressed Fan.

"She's not little!" Don said protectively, putting his arm around his sister. "And she's not your lass, neither. She's our lass."

"She's too young for school," Cyril added. "Pappa won't let her go."

"Don! Cyril! My boys must not be rude," reproved Marcia.

The boys apologized, and then Marcia sent them to run and play.

"They're pretty children," remarked Miss Drybread as the boys disappeared.

"Very frank in the expression of their sentiments and wishes, sometimes," Wealthy said.

"How do you like Pleasant Plains?" Miss Drybread asked.

The question was addressed more particularly to Wealthy, and it was she who replied.

"We are quite disposed to like the place, Miss Stalebread. The streets are widely pleasant and would be quite beautiful if the forest trees had been left."

"Drybread!" the woman corrected. "A good, honest name; if not quite so aristocratic and fine sounding as Keith."

"Pardon me!" said Wealthy. "I have an unfortunate memory for names and had no intention of miscalling yours."

"Oh. Then it's all right." She smiled, and her face was almost pretty. "Mrs. Keith, I'm a teacher; I take young girls of all ages. Perhaps you might entrust me with some of yours? I see you have quite a flock."

"I will take it into consideration." Marcia returned her smile. "What subjects do you teach?"

"Art and music, embroidery, manners…everything that is proper for a young lady to learn. The school is not far from here, and within easy walking distance of your home."

"You don't feel girls could benefit from lessons in history, mathematics, and science?" Millie asked.

"Whatever for?" Miss Drybread seemed surprised.

"To make use of the brains God gave them," Millie said, remembering the fun she'd had in Mr. Martin's class. She was all set to continue, reproducing one of his famous speeches, but Marcia gave her a look.

"I will certainly consider your school," Marcia said. "But I should speak to my husband first."

As the Keiths walked home, they discussed the service and the pleasant people they had met. Zillah and Adah were eager to go to school to make new friends, but Stuart was not easily convinced.

"These years are very important to your future education," he said. "I want you to learn arithmetic, history, botany, and every subject your heads can hold!"

"But there is no other school here, Pappa," Zillah reasoned.

"And we will meet all of the girls!" Adah pleaded. "Please, Pappa!"

Stuart finally agreed that he would make arrangements for Zillah and Adah to start with Miss Drybread the very

next morning. Fan was too young for school, and Millie too advanced for any classes Miss Drybread offered.

After the children had been changed from their Sunday best, the family had a cold dinner of sandwiches and pickles. "My dear," Stuart said as they were finishing the meal, "several days ago, I asked you to take a walk with me. Will you take another now?"

"Of course," said Marcia.

"And us, too?" asked Don.

"I wouldn't leave without you," Stuart said.

Once more Rupert became the marshal of the family. This time as their walk took them through the town, people they had met in church smiled and waved. Millie smiled back and called hello to several girls. Stuart stopped on a hill high above the town overlooking the valley and the river. There were several ancient oaks standing guard on the hill, grand old trees that had seen the storms of centuries.

"What a beautiful spot, Stuart!" Marcia exclaimed. "What views! I haven't seen the whole area at once like this."

"It gives you a feeling of grandeur," Millie said, "to look out over the land from here, doesn't it?" In one direction, she could see the river, rippling in the sun; in the other the growing town stretched out before them. If she were a princess, this is where her castle would sit, high above the town, almost touching the clouds, with the gnarled old trees standing like sentinels day and night.

"Do you really like it?" Stuart asked, drawing Marcia close.

"I do," Marcia replied.

"I believe you've said that to me before, my dear," he teased.

"And I meant every word!" she laughed.

"Then I will build you a house right here."

"Really, Stuart?" Marcia spun around, taking in the view.

"I mean every word," Stuart said. "I am confident enough to spend some of the funds we received from our old house on the purchase of this land. We can't afford to start building just yet, but when the house is finished, we'll be able to see the Kankakee Marsh from the second story windows."

"Marsh?" Wealthy asked in a tone of alarm. "How far off is it?"

"We're about two miles from this end; it is two hundred miles long, you know, extending far over into Illinois. Why?"

"Ague!"

"Bless you," Millie said, coming out of her castle daydream.

"Ague is not a sneeze," Marcia explained. "It's a terrible sickness. A fever. It comes off the marshes and swamps in the air. We never had it in Lansdale, as there were no swamps."

"We'll cross that bridge when we come to it," Stuart said. "This is a beautiful spot. I think we can make it more lovely than our gardens in Lansdale."

"I think so, too, if we can keep these fine old oaks," said Marcia.

"We'll manage our building in a way not to interfere with them," Stuart assured her. "Our grandchildren will climb them."

"How soon can the house be done?" Millie asked, a little alarmed at the talk of grandchildren. Surely they would not have to wait that long!

"Better to ask how soon it will be begun," laughed her father. "If we get into it by next spring we may consider ourselves fortunate."

"Oh," groaned Cyril, Don, and Fan with one accord.

"The time will slip around before you know it, dears," said Aunt Wealthy cheerily.

"And we'll get this ground fenced in. You can spend your time digging and planting and planning," said Stuart.

"May I help plan the house?" asked Ru.

Stuart smiled. "You may," he said. "It will be the Keith house—not the parents' only, but the children's too."

"Then I want to plan the gardens," Millie said. "I think a swing would be perfect under that giant of a tree."

"That is a wonderful idea," Stuart said. "Millie's swing will be the first thing we build!"

Stuart bought rope and a sturdy board for a seat the very next morning. Millie and Ru were excused from watching the children. Rupert made holes in the board, and together they walked through town and up the hill. Ru shimmied up into the tree, and Millie threw him both ropes. While he tied the ropes to the branches, Millie threaded them through the holes in the board seat and tied a fat knot so that they couldn't pull out. When it was finished, Millie had the first turn, pumping her legs and leaning until the swing rose high above the branch, pausing for a breathless moment before it rushed back down. She could see the swamp in the distance, and houses and fields, all of Pleasant Plains at a glance, and then it was gone. Millie sat on the swing long after Ru had lost interest and wandered away. It was the first thing in Pleasant Plains that was really, truly hers.

CHAPTER

13

A Bible Study

*Have I now become your enemy
by telling you the truth?*

GALATIANS 4:16

A Bible Study

"*M*amma, what do you think?" Millie twirled to show off her fresh skirt and apron. Aunt Wealthy had plaited her golden hair in two braids along her head, and Millie had chosen a pretty hat that set off her blue eyes.

"I think my daughter looks every inch the lady," Marcia said. "And I am proud to have her represent the Keiths at a Bible study."

"All that's lacking is the Bible," Millie laughed. She ran upstairs to her bedside table and picked up her Bible. The pages showed the wear and tear of constant use, but Aunt Wealthy had made a clever slipcover for the book out of boards, fabric, and paste to keep it together a little longer. Millie slipped it into her black satin reticule.

"Lord," Millie prayed, "I know it takes time to become friends. But let me start to find a friend today!"

Claudina Chetwood met her at the door of a lovely brick home, and ushered her inside. The house smelled of wax and wood polish, and every rail and table top gleamed. The fluted curtains that hung over large windows were stiff with starch, each fold perfect. Millie smiled. It felt like home—like the lovely homes of her friends in Lansdale. Claudina led the way into a pleasant room full of girls ranging in age from twelve to sixteen. Millie was instantly the center of attention as Claudina introduced her.

"How nice to have a new girl in town," said Helen Monocker, the oldest girl present. "And we hear your father has purchased a lovely piece of land on which to build."

"Yes," Millie said, "though it seems a little far from the center of town."

"Not everyone can live in the original neighborhoods," Helen said. "But you must admit, it will be an improvement over a warehouse."

Millie blinked, but before she could reply, Claudina cut in.

"We were just discussing the new fashion in skirts," she said. "We are so far behind times here. Were you very current in Lansdale?"

Millie was uncomfortable with all the attention, but she thought of Bea and smiled. "Some of us were more current than others, I suppose," she said. "But you don't seem at all backward to me."

"I should hope not," Helen smoothed her skirt. "Mother orders the latest from Chicago. But more petticoats are needed to achieve the new look."

"Alice Winston certainly achieved a look at her party last month," Lucilla said, laughing. "I don't know what she was thinking!"

The attention of the group turned suddenly away from Millie, but this new train of conversation made her more uncomfortable than the last.

"Well, I do!" Helen said. "Emma says Alice has been sweet on him forever. She said Mrs. Gilligut told her that Alice writes him letters every day."

Several of the girls giggled.

Millie began to feel very uncomfortable, and Lucilla noticed at once.

"Oh, Millie," she said. "I apologize! How rude of us. You weren't at the party, and know nothing of these people!"

"I'm sure Millie enjoys an intrigue as much as the rest of us," Helen said. "I love Emma's tales!"

Millie bit her lip. If she were in Lansdale, she would have quoted Pappa: "Repeating second-hand knowledge is hearsay

in the courts of man, and gossip in the courts of heaven. I don't want to be guilty of either!" She wasn't in Lansdale with her friends, though. She was an invited guest in a new place. But wasn't right right and wrong wrong no matter where you were? And God's Word was very clear about gossip.

"I think…" Millie began, but at that moment Mrs. Chetwood came out to offer the sandwiches and lemonade she had prepared. She encouraged the girls to start on the verse at hand as soon as they were finished eating. Millie was relieved, but a little ashamed of herself for not finishing her sentence. She gratefully accepted a sandwich, but left her lemonade untouched.

When the dishes were removed, Claudina cleared her throat and tapped her glass with a spoon. The other girls giggled at her, but it was time to begin, and it did seem that several girls were actually ready to study.

Claudina began with prayer, remembering each of their families, and particularly the Keiths.

"We will be studying the sixteenth chapter of First Samuel today, starting at the seventh verse," she said.

Millie opened her reticule and pulled out her Bible.

"How… quaint," Helen said. "I've never seen a Bible quite like that before."

"Oh," Millie knew she was blushing, but couldn't help it. "My Aunt made this cover for me. The Bible is worn, you see." She slipped off the cover and showed the tattered cover.

Several of the girls looked at each other.

"It must be very old," Helen said, "to look like that. Won't your father buy you a new one?"

"Oh, no. I mean, of course Pappa would, if I asked him." Millie tried to smile. "I like this one, even if it is well used."

"I've never heard of anyone wearing out a Bible before," Helen said. "My grandmother has gone to church every single Sabbath of her life, and her Bible looks like new!"

"I'm sure she's very careful with it," Millie said, flushing even redder.

"Could you read the verse for us, Millie?" Claudina asked.

Millie smiled her thanks, and flipped quickly to the verse.

"'The Lord does not look at things the way man does,'" she read. "'Man looks at the outward appearance, but the Lord looks at the heart.' And thank goodness for that!" Millie added.

"Actually, I find that verse confusing," Lucilla said. "I'm sure the Lord can look at a heart. But why did God put it in the Bible if we can't look at hearts? We only see the outside of people. How else are we to choose our friends if not by how they dress and behave? I mean, rules of behavior and appearance are so important, don't you think?"

"I completely agree with you, Lu. This verse is talking about what God does, not what we should do," Helen said. "Appearance is important. I would no more wear something inappropriate to church or to a social than I would quack like a duck!"

"Aren't we supposed to do just as Jesus would do?" Millie asked.

"Of course," several voices agreed.

"Didn't Jesus say He did what He saw His Father doing? Right here in John 10:37." Millie flipped to the verse and read, "'Do not believe me unless I do what my Father does.' Doesn't that imply that we should try to look at things the way God does?"

"Are you saying we should not dress well and do our hair?" Lu asked.

"That's begging the point," Claudina said. "This verse isn't saying we mustn't wash our faces and brush our hair one hundred strokes. I think it implies that we must not think less of people who do things differently."

"Shouldn't our motivation always be to bring honor to our Lord? In our dress, our manner, our actions and words...in all we do, shouldn't we strive to please God?" Millie asked. The girls were clearly listening to her intently, or she would have stopped right there. "Of course I want my outward appearance to be neat and clean. But I want God to look at my heart, and to see something beautiful there. My mother is the most beautiful woman I have ever known, even when she is tired and her hair is messy. She has taught me what inner beauty is—the kind of beauty that will last a lifetime. That matters so much more than where you live or what you wear."

"It's understandable that you should feel that way," Helen asked.

"What do you mean?" Millie asked, but a hush fell over the group as Mrs. Chetwood entered the sunporch carrying a tray with more lemonade and tea cakes for dessert. She quickly retreated, smiling at the girls as she went.

"I think our outward appearance, the appearance of a lady, is very important," Helen said, when she was gone. "Of course, it is most likely different for those who are not in our social circle. The lower classes, for example...the less educated...well, you know, it must be simply dreadful for them, but that is just how it is. Perhaps God was looking at their hearts when he gave them their humble circumstances. Perhaps they don't deserve any more. After all,

everybody has their place, even if they long to leave it. Or do people in Ohio have a differing opinion?"

Millie felt her face growing hot again.

"Really, Helen, you can be such a snob," said Lu. "Not all servants are in dire straits. I imagine it's possible they are quite content in their world. Take Rhoda Jane Lightcap, for example. She is the most stubborn-headed girl I have ever known. I doubt she misses a minute of our parties and socials."

"Do you mean that she isn't invited or that she chooses not to attend?" Millie asked.

Claudina blushed this time. "You've not met Rhoda Jane, Millie. Her family lives just up the street from you. I'm sure you've noticed their shop. Mr. Lightcap was a blacksmith in our little town until he fell ill and died."

"Their house is not nearly as…big as yours, Millie," Lu said. "Their house is hardly more than a shack. And their mother doesn't have time for the church because she's so busy taking in washing to keep the wolf from the door. It's a shame really, because Gordon is so handsome. I wish he were a gentleman!"

Helen laughed and said, "Gordon Lightcap as a gentleman? It's too funny!"

"I'm afraid I don't understand," said Millie. "The mother works hard to feed her family. And the son, Gordon? If he is of good character, then isn't he a gentleman already?"

"People from Ohio seem to have very progressive ideas," Helen said. "But they may find they have progressed in the wrong direction!"

Claudina stood up, barely hiding her embarrassment. "Girls, I have to say that today's Bible study was of little value. At the very least, we should stay focused on the

Scripture at hand, which was, as I recall, about the important difference between outward appearances and what's in one's heart!"

Lu and Helen stared first at Claudina and then at Millie.

"What did I say?" Lu asked. "I am sorry if I spoke out of turn or offended anyone here. Though I do think I have a right to my opinion." She and Helen both stood to leave. Everyone said their good-byes, but Millie could barely speak. Her tears were too near falling.

When the other girls had left, she turned to Claudina.

"I am so sorry," she said. "It was a perfectly lovely afternoon and I spoiled it."

"I will admit we have never had a Bible study quite like that before," Claudina said. "But I don't think you said anything wrong. How can you study the Bible and not speak the truth? Besides, I know Helen and Lu. They will have forgotten about it by tomorrow." She walked Millie to the door.

"I want to apologize to you, Millie," she said. "I knew you were right, and I didn't stand up for you. I am so envious of your courage!"

"I was afraid to truly speak my mind," Millie confessed. "If my temper hadn't flared, I might not have. My friends in Lansdale would have chided me for that."

"Do you miss your friends?" Claudina asked.

"More than I can say."

Claudina linked arms with Millie as they walked down the steps. "How about this? I will pray for you, Millie Keith, to make new friends who will chide you daily about your temper. And you pray for me to have more courage to speak to my old friends."

"Oh, is it over already?" Mrs. Chetwood said, coming out onto the porch. "How was the study?"

"Terribly wonderful," said Millie.

"Wonderfully terrible," said Claudina, and they both burst out laughing.

As she walked home in the warm, clear sunshine, Millie paused when she saw the hand-lettered sign over the Lightcaps' shop and house. She couldn't help but wonder about Rhoda Jane and Gordon. She was sure they hadn't been at church. She didn't remember seeing the little girls at church, either. In Lansdale all of her friends had lived in neat brick homes in tree-lined neighborhoods. Had she known any poor people? What would she have thought if a girl who lived in a warehouse had come to her Bible study? Her thoughts were interrupted by a shout.

"Hello! Is this here the Keith house?" The girl's face was sun-browned, and she was hardly taller than Zillah. She wore a man's hat on her head. Her dress was shabby, but clean, and she appeared to be wearing a pair of men's overalls underneath instead of pantalets or petticoats.

"Yes," Millie said, extending her hand to the girl, "this is the Keith house. I'm Millie Keith."

"Yes'm," the girl replied, as she grasped Millie's offered hand in a firm grip and jerked it up and down like a pump handle. "My name is Celestia Ann Huntsinger and I come to work for your ma. Don't mistake me for my size. I can heft a cow, if I need to."

"We do have a cow," Millie said. "But I don't think she needs hefting. Won't you come in?"

Celestia Ann pulled off her hat at the doorstep, and Millie almost gasped. Her red hair was short, and as tangled as a

bird's nest. The girl saw Millie's look, and ran her hands over it.

"Too tangled to brush out," she said. "I guess I should have the barber chop it off, but I'm that picky about my head. Don't like anyone touching it. I'm a Christian, ma'am, and I thank the Lord for my red hair every day. Thank You!" she said, waving her hat at the sky, "In case I fergot!" And then in a whisper to Millie, "But it seems He could have made it less tangly."

Millie could only nod.

"When Mrs. Prior over to the Union told me you folks wanted a girl, I knew it was the good Lord's doin'," Celestia Ann said, squinting. "She said you was real Christian folk, and I can see it on you."

Millie almost laughed. Did the Lord have a sense of humor? Meeting Celestia Ann on the doorstep right after that prayer meeting...

"Celestia Ann, how old are you?" Millie asked as she opened the front door.

"Jes' turned seventeen years, ma'am. Why?"

"Because I have not yet turned thirteen years of age and since you are older, I think you ought to call me Millie, not 'ma'am'."

"Yes, ma'am, I'll do that. Thank you kindly, ma'am." Millie smiled and shook her head as Celestia Ann crossed the threshold of the Keiths' home.

If Marcia and Aunt Wealthy were taken aback by Celestia Ann's appearance, they showed no sign of it. Marcia interviewed the girl, asking about her previous experience and references before she hired her.

Aunt Wealthy showed her the small room they had curtained off in the back of the kitchen for her. Celestia Ann ran her hands over the goose-down pillow and touched the oil lamp by her bed.

"It's as good as a palace," she declared, "and I'm glad to have it."

Millie had liked Celestia Ann from the moment she saw her. She was not surprised to hear that Mamma and Aunt Wealthy were of the same opinion. The very first day Celestia Ann proved herself a hard worker and a good cook. Cyril, Don, and Fan were mesmerized by the stories of Indians and wild animals that she spun effortlessly as she cooked. When Millie told her about the Indians they had met, Celestia Ann explained that they weren't permanent neighbors at all, just resting a few weeks as they passed through. The U.S. government was moving them all away. Celestia Ann, in turn, listened open-mouthed while Millie explained the reason the Keiths used only honey or maple sugar to sweeten their food. "You seen this all in print?" Celestia Ann asked. Millie produced the paper and read the article aloud. "I never knowed it. I will never touch a drop of sugar myself again. Never! To treat human be-uns like they was animals! That's wrong before God!"

After the table was set, Marcia invited Celestia Ann to sit with them during supper, but she was up and down the whole time bringing dishes from the kitchen and taking plates away.

"You are very quiet this evening," Stuart said, patting Zillah's head after dessert. "How were your studies today?"

Adah looked at Zillah, and Zillah looked at her plate. "I'm at the head of the class in spelling," she said.

"That's wonderful!" Aunt Wealthy said. "And how about you, Adah?"

Adah paused for a moment before she answered. "I like the girls," she said at last.

"You two look exhausted," Aunt Wealthy said. "Studying and playing must be hard work."

"Yes," said Adah. "I am very tired."

"And how were my boys today?" Stuart asked. "The climate was certainly amenable to outdoor activities."

Celestia Ann's fork paused in mid air.

"He means we're having nice weather," Millie explained.

"Powerful nice," Celestia Ann agreed. "When the good Lord sends us a sweet cool spell in summer, like this un here, a body ain't even got a fightin' chance of breakin' a sweat! We all oughta thank Him good."

"Amen, Miss Huntsinger," Stuart said. "Amen!"

CHAPTER 14

New Experiences

*Do not forget to entertain strangers,
for by so doing, some people have
entertained angels without
knowing it.*

HEBREWS 13:2

New Experiences

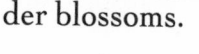

*I*n a little over a week, Celestia Ann Huntsinger was well on her way to becoming a full-fledged member of the Keith family. Marcia cut down one of Millie's old dresses for her, and Aunt Wealthy found one of hers that would just fit the girl. Millie even persuaded the girl to let her tease the knots out of her hair. Celestia Ann would only sit still for this in the evenings, while the family gathered to hear Stuart or Marcia read, so the project took almost the full week, but the result was amazing: an elf-like sprite with a halo of red curls to match her freckles.

Not only was Celestia Ann a very diligent worker, but proud of her talents, too. She loved to show Millie how things were 'done on the frontier,' but if she found that Marcia, Wealthy, or Millie had done some small chore that she considered part of her job, her feelings were hurt.

Marcia had more time to spend with the younger children, and Millie had more time to spend with friends. One day, Millie found herself lying flat on a quilt in the fading summer twilight. She and Claudina had spent the afternoon together on the Keiths' hilltop, swinging and twining flowers in their hair. The early evening was alive with the noise of crickets and a lonely frog by the well. The scent of grass and flowers mingled with the delicious smell of Celestia Ann's blackberry cobbler cooling on the kitchen windowsill.

The girls were exhausted but happy. Millie's twin braids were now fastened with blue ribbons and cheerful daisies; Claudina's long dark curls wore a wreath of delicate lavender blossoms.

"Do you know that this spot is lovely in the gloaming?" Millie asked.

"I might agree with you, if I knew what a 'gloaming' was," Claudina said.

Millie smiled, but it was a sad smile. Camilla would have known what the gloaming was. Claudina was fast becoming a friend, but Millie still missed discussing books and ideas and dreams for the future more than she could say. And though she wrote letters to her friends faithfully each week, the ones she received in reply were few and far between.

"The gloaming is the twilight just before dark," Millie said. "When the shadows all turn purple."

"Oh, why didn't you just say that? Of course it's lovely then."

"In the gloaming," Millie said dreamily. "It's lovely in the gloaming."

"If you keep filling your head with words from books, Millie Keith, you will have no time for fun. Have your parents decided if you can go to Beth's party?"

Millie had received the invitation two days before. Beth Roe was holding a rag-rolling party and all of the young ladies in the neighborhood were invited. They would work all afternoon making rag balls to be used for making rugs, and of course Mamma and Pappa would have no objection to that; but after the work was done, the young men were invited for games and dessert.

"Pappa said he was sure that the Roes are respectable," Millie said. "And he was sure that my behavior would be impeccable."

"Are you serious!" Claudina said. "You can come?"

Millie nodded. "I must confess, I am a little nervous. The last time I appeared in public it was a disaster."

New Experiences

Claudina threw a daisy at her, and Millie smiled.

"Honestly," Millie said, "I haven't seen Helen or Lu since your ill-fated Bible study, except at church."

"Oh," Claudina lay back down, "you should have no fear then. You won't see Helen or Lu at a rag-rolling party. The Roes are not cultivated people, or very refined, but they're good folks and kind neighbors. If there is trouble or sickness they are the first ones to offer help. I'm so glad your parents are letting you go. The Roes would be dreadfully hurt if you should decline their invitation."

"What time does one arrive for a rag party?" Millie asked, as the girls rose and began walking home.

"We are invited to work, you know," said Claudina, laughing, "so we will be expected early, no later than one o'clock, I think. And it's not very nice work—carpet rags are apt to be dusty—so you shouldn't wear anything that will not wash. I'm wearing a calico dress and carrying a big work apron with me, and bringing my own sewing basket."

"Then I'll do the same. And I'm sure Celestia Ann will come. She's invited too, you know."

The girls arrived at the Big Yellow House and sat outside near the shed, admiring Belle and chatting gaily until it was time for Claudina to leave.

Suddenly, Zillah called from the back door, "Millie! The Indians are coming!"

Millie and Claudina hurried to the back door and in through the kitchen.

"The Indians ain't comin'," Celestia Ann said, as they passed through the kitchen. "The Indians are here!"

And they were indeed, standing in the dining room, and the sitting room, filling the open door, spilling out into the

front yard and the street. Tall men with still faces, women with little children, and tiny babies with dark, solemn eyes.

Wealthy was speaking French with the man who appeared to be their leader.

"He's the one that gave us the berries," Zillah said. "And there's his wife!"

Millie looked through the front window and gasped. The street in front of their house was full of Indians, some on horseback, some on foot.

"His name is Pe-pe-ne-way," Wealthy said. "The government agent told them they have to leave. He said Millie invited him to meet her parents."

Millie stepped forward and spoke in her best French, "Welcome to our house."

He nodded, then spoke too quickly for her to understand. She looked despairingly at Wealthy.

"He said good-bye, and that you will not see them again. The U.S. government says they must go west, west of the Mississippi, where there are fewer white people."

"They're walkin' the whole way? The poor things! They look tuckered already!" said Celestia Ann. She was past Millie in a flash and out on the porch. She made her way through the Potawatami people to the well and started cranking.

"Can we get cups, Mamma?" Millie asked.

"Good thinking," Marcia said. "Hurry now."

The young Keiths rushed to the kitchen for the cups, and by the time Celestia Ann had pulled the bucket of water up, they were waiting.

She filled the cups from the dipper, and the children carried them to the waiting people, offering cool well water in fine china cups to everyone who was thirsty.

The Indians were of all ages, from ancient warriors to babies tied into little wooden troughs that the mothers

stood up on end on the ground. The babies were very quiet, and all you could see of them were their little round faces and dark eyes. They were wrapped in cloth that pinned their arms and legs, with nothing to amuse them but a string of tiny bells across the trough in front of their faces.

The horses dragged travois behind them, full of bundles wrapped in hides and blankets. One travois was the bed of an ancient warrior. Millie stopped to offer him a drink, but he turned his face away from her and closed his eyes. A tiny old woman spoke to him sternly, but still he wouldn't accept the drink.

Aunt Wealthy was standing on the front porch, watching, and as the people drank, she started to speak. Her French was smooth and beautiful, but Millie couldn't follow it all.

"What is she saying, Mamma?" Millie whispered when she went back to the porch.

"She's telling them about Jesus," her mother said quietly.

The Indians listened politely until she was done, and then Pe-pe-ne-way spoke.

"He says that he's heard of this Jesus before, and believes he is a powerful God. He says that if we are friends of Jesus, we should ask Him to help the Potawatami. Their own friends have left them, and their life is leaving them, too. He is asking us to pray for them."

Wealthy bowed her head and prayed, and there were tears running down her cheeks. Then Pe-pe-ne-way nodded his head, turned, and walked away. His people followed him down the street. The Keiths watched until they disappeared.

Millie could hardly touch her supper that night.

"Where are the babies going to sleep, Pappa?" Zillah asked. "Will they have houses west of the Mississippi? What will they eat?"

"They will have to make houses," Stuart said. "And they will eat deer and fish and berries."

"At least there won't be white people there, puttin' up fences and kicking them from one place to the next," Celestia Ann said.

"Not yet," said Stuart. "Not yet."

That night at bedtime, they prayed for the Indians again.

The next day, Millie dressed for the rag party in her oldest calico dress and a huge work apron.

"Oh, you're beautiful," Celestia Ann exclaimed when she saw her. "Girl, you could dress in a feed sack and still look like an angel!"

Millie thanked her for the compliment, yet she couldn't help but wonder what her old friends would think of this party dress, or of her leaving home with the maid to attend the same party.

"Don't worry, Millie," Celestia Ann said as they walked down the path. "I'll show you just what to do."

A dozen young ladies, mostly under twenty years of age, were collected in "the front room" at the Roe's house. Millie knew most of them from church, except one pretty girl perhaps a year older than herself, wearing a thin, worn dress. She knew she had seen her before, but couldn't place her until Celestia Ann shouted, "Rhoda Jane! I'm glad as that to see you up and about!"

It was Emmaretta and Minerva's sister, and Millie had seen her the day the cow ran away. She remembered Rhoda Jane's shy smile, and was ashamed that she had been thinking so much of her own embarrassment that she hadn't smiled back. She smiled now, but Rhoda Jane merely nodded.

 180

A large basket filled with many colored rags, torn or cut into strips of various lengths, was set in the middle of the floor. A number of girls were grouped about it, armed with needles and thread, scissors and thimbles. Millie watched for a moment as they picked out the strips, sewed the ends together, and wound the long strips into balls. Some girls had filled their aprons with rags and seated themselves here and there about the room. They seemed a very merry company, laughing and chatting as they worked.

"Oh, how d'ye do?" said Beth, catching sight of Millie. "Thought you wasn't comin' at all." She leaned close to Millie and whispered, "Sorry about that at the butcher's. Ma didn't know you were regular folk, but Mrs. Prior said you was." And then more loudly, "Let me take your hat. Here's a seat for you 'long side of Miss Chetwood. Guess you're better acquainted with her than anybody else."

"Ladies, this is Miss Keith and Celestia Ann."

"I don't need no introduction," laughed Celestia Ann. "'Ope you're well, Miss Beth."

The others looked up with a nod and a murmured word or two, as Beth named each in turn. Then they seemed to take up their conversation where it had been dropped, while Millie tied on her apron and took the chair assigned her. She threaded a needle and helping herself, by invitation, from Claudina's lap, began her first ball.

"Are we all here now?" asked someone.

"All but Damaris Drybread. She's oldish for the rest of us, but she's the schoolmarm, you know, and likes to be invited. She works dreadful fast when she does get at it."

"Pshaw! I wish she hadn't been asked. She spoils everything. She's as solemn as a funeral and 'pears to think it's a sin to laugh."

181

"Yes," added another voice, "that's so and she never forgets that she's a schoolmarm, but takes it upon herself to tell you your duty without waiting to be invited to."

"Hush!" Beth said. "That's her now."

"Good afternoon," Damaris Drybread said in solemn tone, addressing the company in general. She made a stiff little bow, then giving her sunbonnet to Beth, she seated herself in a bolt upright manner and fell to work.

The laughter went out of the room like the light of a lantern that was turned down. Millie studied Damaris's face. How could her mere presence be such a damper? Perhaps if they gave her a chance, she would join the fun.

"I wonder," Millie said loudly, "if any of you know which territory is mentioned in the Bible?"

"There weren't no territories then, nor states neither," Beth laughed, "so none could be mentioned."

"Oh!" Millie said, feigning surprise. "I must have misread it. I thought it said, "Noah looked out of the ark and saw...'"

"Arkansas!" they yelled.

"Who's the shortest man in the Bible?"

"Zacchaeus?" someone guessed.

"Bildad. He was just a Shu-hite."

"I thought it was Nee-high-miah," Claudina said, and everyone laughed.

She glanced at Damaris again. The schoolmarm's face had become even more grave. But the smiles were returned and everyone giggled as Claudina and one or two others began telling jokes, too.

"I declare I haven't laughed so hard since hens grew teeth!" Celestia Ann said at last.

The laughter died again as Miss Drybread spoke. "Permit me to observe to you all that life is too serious and

solemn to be spent in laughing and joking. Allow me to say, Miss Keith, that I am astonished that you, a church member, should indulge in such frivolity."

"Do you think a Christian should always wear a long face?" asked Millie.

"I think that folks who claim to be religious ought to be grave and sober, and let the world see that they don't belong to it."

"But surely there is no harm in laughter," Millie said, "and if anybody in the world has a right to be happy, wouldn't it be the ones who know that Jesus loves them?"

"There is a season for all things," Damaris Drybread said, drawing herself up. "And I believe it is unseemly to laugh and joke when people are suffering and dying."

"People are getting married and being born too," Rhoda Jane said, almost defiantly. "Flowers are bursting into bloom, and breezes are whispering."

"You are hardly an expert on religion," Damaris countered.

"That is true," Rhoda Jane said. "I, for one, want none of your long-faced, sour-looking religion!"

"But," Millie said, "the Bible is full of commands to God's people to rejoice, to be glad, to sing for joy, and the best Christians I know are the happiest people on earth."

"You're rather young to set yourself up as the judge of who's the best Christian," returned Damaris condescendingly. "Don't you think?"

"No, I don't think so at all," Millie replied. "Jesus said, 'By their fruits you will know them.' When I see people serving God with gladness, walking in His ways, rejoicing in His love, and making the Bible always their rule of faith and practice, I think I can be safe in saying they are Christians."

"I think so, too!" said Claudina emphatically. She looked startled, then a little pleased.

"So do I." "And I," chimed in several other voices.

"And you know these people?" Damaris asked. "I'm sure we would all like to meet them."

"Of course," Millie said. "I'm talking about my father and mother. And dear Aunt Wealthy, too."

"That's a fact," spoke up Celestia Ann. "You 'ave to live with folks to find 'em out, and I've lived there and I never seen better Christians. They don't keep their religion for Sundays, but Mr. Keith 'e reads in the good book every night and mornin' and prays just like a minister—only not so long—and they sing 'ymns. And I never 'eard a cross word pass between Mr. and Mrs. or Miss Stanhope neither, and they never threaten the children that they'll do something awful like breakin' their bones or skinnin' 'em alive, as some folks do; but just speaks to 'em quiet-like, sayin' exactly what they mean. And they're always minded, too."

"There had better be less talk and more work if these rags are all to be sewed today," remarked Miss Drybread, taking a fresh supply from the basket, then straightening herself till she was, if possible, more erect than before.

"I can talk and work too; my needle haint stopped because my tongue was runnin'," said Celestia Ann, "and it strikes me you've been doin' your share of gabbin' as well's the rest."

CHAPTER

15

A Special Gift

See how the lilies of the field grow. They do not labor or spin, yet I tell you that not even Solomon in all his splendor was dressed like one of these.

<small>MATTHEW 6:28-29</small>

A Special Gift

My second ball's done," said Claudina, tossing it up.

"A good one too, and wound tight," said Beth, giving it a squeeze, then rolling it into a corner where quite a pile had collected.

"How can you roll so quickly, Claudina?" Millie asked, hoping to change the mood.

"I've been at it quite a while. But some here can make two to my one." She glanced toward Miss Drybread, who was just beginning to wind her second.

"I suggest a contest," Millie said, "and the prize will be my silver thimble!"

The young ladies began to stitch and wind with determination. Millie focused on stitching her fabric into long strips. She had quite a pile of them tangled on her lap when she looked up.

"I'd begin to wind if I were you, Millie," Claudina laughed, "or your thimble is lost!"

"That's three!" Damaris Drybread said, tossing a ball into the corner.

"Four," Rhoda Jane said, throwing one right after it.

Damaris gave her a grim look, and her fingers flew.

Rhoda Jane smiled and stretched, then picked up another rag. She looked relaxed, but her fingers were moving just as fast as Miss Drybread's, if not faster.

"I think my thimble is already lost," Millie whispered, leaning close to Claudina.

They worked in silence, each intent on her own ball.

"Supper's ready," announced Mrs. Roe, opening the kitchen door.

"Put down your rags, ladies," said Beth.

"Five!" Damaris said triumphantly, holding up her final ball of rags.

"Six." Everyone turned to look at Rhoda Jane, who was also holding up her last ball.

"I believe you have won," Damaris said sourly.

"I believe I have." Rhoda Jane smiled.

"Celestia Ann, why haven't you been throwin' your rags in the corner?" Beth asked. "You have a pile!"

"Din't want to waste time countin' till the rollin' was done," the girl said with a mischievous smile. There were rag balls scattered in her lap and at her feet. "It appears it's done now." She picked up a ball and tossed it in the corner.

"One," she said. By the time she reached four, the whole room was counting with her. "Five…," Damaris and Rhoda Jane exchanged a look. " Six. Seven. Eight!"

"All nice-sized and tightly-wrapped too," Beth announced.

The girls cheered as Millie gave Celestia Ann her thimble and a hug.

"Now it's time for supper," Beth said.

"It seems that I, for one, need some preparation," said Millie, looking at her hands.

"Oh, yes, we'll wash out here," said Beth, leading the way.

A tin bucket full of water, a dipper and washbasin, all bright from a recent scouring, stood on a bench in the shed at the outer kitchen door. A piece of brown soap lay there also, and a clean wash towel hung on a nail on the wall close by. The girls used these in turn, laughing and chatting merrily all the while.

When they gathered about the table, they found it bountifully spread with good plain country fare—chicken, ham,

dried beef, pickles, tomatoes, cucumbers and radishes, cheese, eggs, pie, cake and preserves in several varieties, hot cakes and cold bread, tea and coffee.

None of the family partook with their guests except Beth. Claudina explained to Millie that they would eat afterwards, when the guests had all had their fill. Mrs. Roe busied herself waiting upon the table, filling the tea and coffee cups in the shed where the cooking stove stood during the months of the year when its heat was objectionable in the house.

"I don't know as we've earned our supper, Miz' Roe," remarked Celestia Ann, stirring her tea. "We hain't begun to git all them rags sewed up yet."

"Well, then, I'll just set you to work again as soon as you're done eating. Folks don't always pay in advance, you know."

"And if we don't finish before the boys come, we'll make them help," said Rhoda Jane.

"Boys don't use needles," Damaris said. Some of the girls giggled.

"I don't see why not," Rhoda Jane said. "They've got fingers. And I think some of them are pretty old to be called boys."

"Yes, that's true," said a girl. "Rod Stuefield must be thirty at least."

"And Nick Ransquate's twenty-five if he's a day," remarked another.

"Well, the rest's young enough," said Mrs. Roe. "Pass that cake there, Rhoda Jane. There's Gordon Lightcap who just turned sixteen, and York Monocker, Wallace Ormsby, my own Joe, and Claudina's brother Bill, are all younger than him."

The meal concluded, the work went on quite briskly again. Millie caught now and then a whispered word or two about getting through with it in time to have some fun. She rose to help Beth and Mrs. Roe carry the dishes to the kitchen. Everyone else was so much quicker at winding the rag balls, she felt she could be of better help there.

"Look!" said Beth, as they deposited a load on the sideboard. "There's Gordon and Joe." Millie followed her gaze. Two young men in rough work clothes were standing outside the window, looking up intently at something above them.

"Joe's the one with the hat," Beth said. "And Gordon's the handsome one!"

Joe glanced in the window, as if he sensed they were talking about him. He made a face at Beth, and tipped his cap to Millie; then lifted one muddy workboot and put it into the stirrup Gordon Lightcap had made out of his hands. Gordon lifted, and Joe practically sailed up out of sight. There was a brief scraping on the wall and a thud above their heads.

"What on earth are they doing?" Millie asked, as Gordon reached up, took hold of something, and walked up the wall like a mountain climber.

"Goin' up to Joe's room to change. Claudina's here," Beth giggled, "and Joe's plum sweet on her. He wants to slick up afore she sees him. Oh!" Beth clapped her hand over her mouth. "I wasn't s'posed to tell nobody that."

"Don't worry," Millie said. "I can keep a secret."

Joe and Gordon appeared in less than half an hour, dropping out of the sky the same way they had gone, quite "slicked up," as Beth elegantly expressed it, though their preparations had been made under difficulty. Their hair

was neatly combed, and their shirts and pants clean and pressed.

Joe tapped on the window.

"My land!" Beth exclaimed, opening the window, "what a time you've been up there. I never knowed you to take half as long to dress before."

"My fingers are all thumbs," Joe said, a hot flush spreading over his sunburnt face when he realized Millie was still in the room. "I can't tie this tie decent noway at all. Pardon, Miss."

"Well, just wait till I can wipe my hands, and I'll do it." Beth wiped her hands then leaned out the window. "There, that'll do. The girls aren't going to look real hard at that bit o' black ribbon."

"Maybe not, but I'm obliged to you all the same for fixin' it right."

The boys decided to wait in the yard until more of the fellows arrived. Millie and Beth went back to their work, finished the dishes and retired to the sitting room. When the young men finally entered, there were three together—Joe, Gordon, and Nicholas Ransquate.

Nicholas was short and thick-set, had scarcely any hair, and moved like a man made of wood. He carried his head thrown back on his shoulders. Even his face was stiff, with large features and a stolid expression. But he was not bashful in the least, and seemed to have no fear that his society would be less than acceptable to anyone he might meet.

"Good evening, ladies. I'm happy to see you all," he said, making a sweeping bow to the company, hat in hand. "And I hope I see you well."

"Well, you seen us," someone quipped, and the girls giggled.

"Good evening," responded several voices more politely.

"Good evenin', Mr. Lightcap." Millie was surprised to hear Celestia Ann's voice.

Gordon glanced at her and smiled.

"Find yourselves seats and we'll give you employment threading our needles for us," Rhoda Jane said, "for I hear your species cannot sew."

Beth introduced Nicholas to Millie, and then managed to seat him on the far side of the room next to Damaris Drybread, upon whom Nicholas bestowed a smile.

"Ah, the charming schoolmarm. May I untangle your rags as you wind?"

"As you wish," Damaris said stoically.

Gordon took an empty chair by his sister's side, and Joe sat by him.

"I guess you never sewed carpet rags before," Joe said to Millie.

"Is it my awkwardness that makes you think so?" Millie asked with a smile.

"No," he said, "you do it...beautiful!" His eyes were fixed on Claudina, whose dark tresses reflected the candle-light as she picked up more rags. "I mean...I...what did you say?"

"Let me give you some work," Millie said, taking pity on his embarrassment. "Will you thread this needle for me?"

"And then mine, please," put in Claudina, who had seated herself on Millie's other side.

Joe struggled with Millie's needle, and then reached for Claudina's. When he returned it she smiled, and to his apparent delight launched into a reminiscence of a candy-pulling they had both attended the year before. Millie was able to sew without saying a word.

A Special Gift

By twos and threes the other "boys" came flocking in. The room was getting crowded, and there was some tossing back and forth of the balls, amid rather loud laughter. But some of them unwound and became entangled, and so that sport was given up and the work put away. The girls washed their hands as they had before supper.

Damaris Drybread situated herself in a corner while the group cleared the floor for Blindman's Bluff. Millie found herself laughing out loud as Nicholas allowed himself to be blindfolded, spun in place, then staggered around the room trying to tag the others as if he were no more than Rupert's age. It was ridiculous and hilarious at the same time, and by the end of the game, the only one not laughing was Damaris Drybread, who had situated herself in a corner and refused all offers to play.

Other games were suggested and played with as much zest as if the revelers had been a group of children. Then refreshments followed, served up in the kitchen.

There was more laughter and stories of other parties as huckleberries with cream and sugar, watermelons, muskmelons, doughnuts, and cupcakes were devoured.

At ten o'clock the party broke up. Nicholas offered to see Celestia Ann and Millie safely home, but Celestia Ann just laughed.

"It's not more than a hop, skip, and a jump," she said. "I don't expect we need mindin'."

As they walked home through the moonlight, Celestia Ann talked about the party and the games, but Millie was thinking about Damaris sitting, stiff and aloof, as everyone played.

Lord, Millie prayed. *Show her Your joy!*

193

Millie's Unsettled Season

"That was the strangest party I have ever been to," Millie confessed the next morning as she helped Mamma with Annis. "Not like a Lansdale party at all."

"Do you miss the gowns and the dances?" her mother asked, with a twinkle in her eye.

"Yes," Millie admitted. "It's not vanity to love dressing up, is it, Mamma?"

"No, not unless you become prideful, or consider others less than yourself."

Millie sighed. "It's too bad there is nothing in Pleasant Plains to dress up for," she said.

"Really?" Marcia asked. "Then I suppose you haven't heard of the Christmas social."

"A social?"

"That's what I hear. In mid-December the whole town is invited to a grand ball. It's three months away, but girls are ordering their dresses already, and fabric is flying off the shelves at the store."

"Mamma, are we going? I could alter the yellow gown I wore last year to Bea's party. It still fits."

"That's true, you haven't grown an inch. But that dress just doesn't suit you anymore."

"What do you mean?"

"I mean," said Marcia, "that you are becoming a young lady. That yellow dress is much too young for you." She pointed to a crate chair. "You might find a package under there, if you were to look."

Millie lifted the crate top and saw a brown paper package. She tore it open to find yards of emerald green silk.

"Oh, Mamma! Where did this come from? I'm sure there is nothing like it in the store!"

"I'm sure there is not. Did you think I would forget that my daughter was turning thirteen in December? I bought it in Lansdale, and have carried it along. And in three months time, we are going to make the most beautiful dress Pleasant Plains has ever seen!"

For the next week they poured over patterns and catalogues that Aunt Wealthy pulled out of nowhere. She also produced a beautiful length of French lace for collar and cuffs. Every detail was planned before scissors ever touched the silk. Marcia measured carefully, suggesting that if Millie wore heels they could leave the skirt long. Then she would be assured of wearing the dress more than once, even if she decided to grow. If she did not, it could always be hemmed. Finally, Aunt Wealthy laid out the pattern and the fabric was cut.

Aunt Wealthy was working on a gown of wine-colored velvet for Celestia Ann, who protested that she would not wear it, but loved to feel the fabric, even so.

It wasn't the same without Bea and Annabeth, but Millie loved sitting up late with Mamma and Aunt Wealthy, with needles busy, talking about everything under the sun.

CHAPTER

16

Another Rescue

Rescue the weak and needy;
deliver them from the hand
of the wicked.

PSALM 82:4

Another Rescue

*T*he leaves on the maples, oaks and sycamores began to turn slowly from every shade of green to gold and russet, orange and scarlet. The air, which had been heavy and hot, gradually grew cooler, and the mornings were quite brisk. Millie's gingham-checked dresses and white pantalets were put away for heavier, darker-colored frocks, and cotton stockings. The carefree, rough and tumble days of summer were seemingly gone overnight, and autumn was upon them.

Rupert spent almost as much of his time at the office with his father as he did working around the house. Adah and Zillah had settled into school, and Cyril, Don, and Fan spent their days exploring with Wannago or pretending to be Indians, and their evenings listening to Bible stories at Pappa's side.

The routine of the Keith household had been restored, even in the Big Yellow House. Marcia had somehow worked the pieces of her life, as a Christian woman, wife, mother of eight, mistress of a growing household, and volunteer to charitable causes, into a beautiful quilt that kept her family warm and safe.

"Make sure the boys and Fan eat something," she told Millie one day as she and Wealthy left for a meeting of the ladies society. "We will be back before the girls return from school."

Millie curled on a cushion in a beam of sunlight, her Bible open on her lap, gazing out the window. She could see Fan sitting with her back to the tree in the yard, and her head on her knees. She looked so much like Zillah. Millie shook her head. Her little sister had become so solemn in the last few weeks since Zillah and Adah had begun school with Damaris Drybread.

Millie remembered Damaris in the corner of the room at the rag party, a look of disapproval on her face. How could she possibly show God's joy and love to the children in her classroom if she did not have it herself? Or was it possible that God expected such solemnity of a teacher?

Millie read the verse before her. "Not many of you should presume to be teachers, my brothers, because you know that we who teach will be judged more strictly," said James 3:1. Perhaps Miss Drybread was so rigid and solemn because she feared being judged. But surely she knew that God was a loving Father! The very next verse, James 3:2, said, "We all stumble in many ways. If anyone is never at fault in what he says, he is a perfect man, able to keep his whole body in check." God knew that no one was perfect, not even a teacher. If He had grace for His children, how much more must He have for those who loved His children and wanted to teach them? Millie was sure God loved Mr. Martin, her beloved teacher in Lansdale, because Mr. Martin obviously loved Him and all of His children.

She shut her Bible and put it on the table by her bed, then gazed once again out the window. Fan was still sitting against the tree, her head on her knees. Was she sad, or missing Zillah and Adah?

Millie walked downstairs and out across the yard. Fan didn't lift her head up.

"Are you sad, kitten?" Millie asked, gathering her skirts and sitting down beside her.

"Yes," Fan said. "I'm mad, too."

"Why are you mad?" Millie asked, surprised.

"Because they tied me to the tree," Fan said.

"Tied!" Millie leaned over. Don's rope was around Fan's waist, hidden by her apron. The knot was behind the tree where the little girl couldn't reach it.

"The wicked rascals!" Millie said, working at the knot. "Why did they tie you up?" Don's knots were getting better. He'd pulled the cords tight, and Millie had to work hard to loosen them.

"Because they went on the warpath, that's why," Fan said, as Millie worked to free her. "They always leave me!"

"On the warpath?"

"Yep," Fan said. "They're gonna rescue Zillah and Adah from the witch."

"Miss Drybread is not a witch. She's just a…a…"

"Adah said she was a witch."

"She did?"

Fan nodded. "And Cyril, he said that he was gonna save Zillah and Adah, cause that's what Jesus would do. And Jesus was brave, and He wouldn't be afraid, even if He wasn't an Indian."

The knots finally came loose, and Fan jumped up. "I'm gonna catch 'em," she said, starting for the path that led over the hill to the schoolhouse.

"Oh, no, you are not." Millie caught her by her apron strings and pulled her back. "I think you need to come talk to Celestia Ann, while I go find Cyril and Don before they get into trouble."

"I want to go, too!"

"Celestia Ann is baking gingerbread," Millie said, "and she might let you lick the bowl. Let's go ask her."

Millie explained the situation briefly to Celestia Ann.

"Good for them," Celestia Ann said, brandishing a wooden spoon. "It warn't my place to say, but if'n I had two little ones like Zillah and Adah, I wouldn't send them to Drybones to learn nothin'!"

"I'm sure Mamma and Pappa wouldn't want us to call her that," Millie said.

"I expect you're right," Celestia Ann said, "but it fits. You want to lick the whole bowl yourself?" she asked Fan.

Fan considered this a moment.

"Can I wear war paint while I lick it?"

"Why not?" asked Celestia Ann. She dabbed a finger in the soot along the rim of the coal bucket, then traced a black line down Fan's nose, and another across her cheeks.

Millie left Fan chattering happily. She walked briskly up the path toward the top of the hill, praying under her breath as she went. What could Adah have meant, calling the teacher such a name? It wasn't like her at all.

She reached the top of the hill, and she could see the schoolhouse across the valley. Smoke curled out of the chimney in the cool of the morning. Millie could just imagine the little scholars inside, safe and sound, not suspecting in the least the excitement that was about to ensue. In fact, it was upon them now, for Cyril and Don had almost reached the school, coonskin caps bobbing as they ran from one bush or rock to another, and ducked for cover.

"Cyriiiil! Don!" Millie called, but she was sure they couldn't hear her. The boys had reached the woodpile beside the school. Cyril climbed up the stack of wood as if it were a staircase, stepped across on the roof and reached down for something Don handed up to him. When Cyril stood up, Millie could see he had a large shake shingle and a rock. He started across the roof, placing his moccasin-clad feet carefully, like a cat.

Another Rescue

Millie didn't realize what he was doing until he reached the chimney. He laid the shingle over the smoking hole and put the rock on top of it to keep it in place, then started back the way he had come.

Millie reached the schoolyard just as they jumped off the woodpile.

"Cyril and Don Keith!" They both whirled. Their faces were striped with berry juice.

"Shhhh!" Cyril said. "They'll hear you."

"I don't care if they do," Millie said. "You go right back up there and take that shingle off the chimney. The whole school will fill with smoke!"

Cyril smiled his gap-toothed smile and nodded. At that moment, the schoolhouse door burst open, and children exploded into the schoolyard, choking and coughing. Smoke poured out of the door behind them.

"What on earth!" Miss Drybread came out last of all, craning her neck to look up at the roof.

"Run, Zillah, Adah!" Don yelled. "Now's your chance!"

Zillah and Adah caught sight of Millie, and did indeed run toward her. Miss Drybread followed.

"Is this your doing?" she demanded. "We will have that shingle off the chimney this instant, and all of my scholars back in school!" She reached for Zillah's hand.

"No, Millie, don't let her take them," Cyril cried. "She's a bad old witch! She said she's gonna burn 'em up in the stove!"

Zillah backed up against Millie's side.

"Is this true?" Millie asked the little girl.

Zillah hid her head in Millie's apron, but Adah said, "Yes."

Miss Drybread's face went very white, and she took a step forward.

203

Cyril and Don, losing their courage, jumped behind Millie, and now all of the little Keiths peeked around her at the woman. What should she do? Surely the teacher was an authority over her sisters. But something was clearly wrong. *Jesus, help me know what to do!* she prayed silently, then squatted and put her arm around her sister.

"What did she say, Zillah?" Millie asked.

"She said she was going to roast to death any child who talks too much," Adah whispered. "She said she was going to build up the fire hot and put them in the stove and cook them!"

"Surely you didn't believe her," Millie said.

"Yes," Zillah said. She was trembling, and Millie could tell she was frightened. "I wasn't afraid for me, Millie, really I wasn't. But Adah is too little to know not to talk!"

"This is nonsense," Miss Drybread said. "I merely said that to keep them quiet in class. Now as soon as that board is removed, we will all return to our studies."

"The board will be removed," Millie said, standing up, "but no Keith is going to return to this classroom."

"Aren't you taking a bit much on yourself again?" Miss Drybread said. "That decision will be made by your parents, I think."

"I am sure that I speak for my parents, for they are very strict about telling lies," Millie said, pulling her sisters close. "Cyril, get back on the roof and remove that shingle."

For once in his life, Cyril ran to obey her. He scrambled back up the woodpile and jumped to the roof, pulled the shingle off, and smoke began to pour out of the chimney once more. Millie gathered her brothers and sisters and started for home, leaving Miss Drybread and her class standing in the schoolyard.

When Marcia came home that afternoon, she found all of her children waiting for her. The story started spilling out of them before she even removed her hat. Fan and Celestia Ann, who had heard it told at least once already, crowded around to hear it again. When the children finished their tale, she gave them all hugs and put her hat right back on.

"I think I need to have a talk with your Pappa," she said.

"We're in really big trouble," Cyril said. "Ain't we?" His face still had red stripes where the berry juice war paint had stained it, and the rest of it was red from trying to scrub it off.

"Boys who take matters into their own hands instead of consulting their pappa can expect to be disciplined," she said. Cyril's face fell, and Don gulped. "But your Pappa is a fair man, and you were trying to save your sister. I don't think you have too much to fear."

It was a solemn afternoon at the Keith house as the children waited for their parents to arrive. It became more solemn still when Stuart and Marcia came home and explained that they had been to see Miss Drybread, and while Adah and Zillah were not going back, Cyril and Don were expected to write letters of apology for calling her such a terrible name.

Stuart took each of the boys aside and spoke to them privately, and then gathered the children together. "It would break my heart if you did not tell me when you have trouble," he said.

If Stuart noticed that when Celestia Ann served the gingerbread for dessert, Cyril and Don not only had the biggest pieces, they had the only pieces with whipped cream and maple sugar, he didn't say a word.

Later that evening, after prayers had been said and children tucked in, Millie sat with her Bible and her oil lamp's warm glow.

"He who desires to be a teacher desires a good thing," she read.

Lord, she prayed silently. *I know I can't do this without You. But You know the desire of my heart. And wouldn't this be a good time to start?* She prayed for a few moments longer, and then went downstairs to the room where her parents and Aunt Wealthy were sitting by the fire.

"Millie!" Stuart said, "I thought you were in bed."

"I was, Pappa." She sat on the couch beside him, pulled up her feet and tucked them into her nightgown. "But I wanted to talk to you and Mamma about what happened today."

He set his reading down.

"I am afraid I did not treat Miss Drybread in a very Christian manner. But I didn't know what to do."

"I think you did very well," Marcia said, sighing. "Miss Drybread has a great deal of knowledge, but…"

" 'Knowledge puffs up, but love builds up'," Wealthy quoted, and sniffed.

"Perhaps she will learn," Marcia said gently. "And one day she will be an excellent teacher."

"That's what I wanted to speak to you about, Mamma," Millie said. "Zillah and Adah shouldn't neglect their studies. I was wondering if…"

"Yes?"

"I want to be their teacher. I know I can teach them reading and sums. And with your help, and Aunt Wealthy's…"

"That's quite a responsibility," Stuart said. "Some people would even say these are the most important years of their education. If they don't learn to love learning…"

"That's just it, Pappa," Millie said earnestly. "I may not have all of the knowledge I need. But I love my sisters. And I love to learn. I think I might make a good teacher."

"I'm very proud of you for asking," Stuart said, wrapping her in a hug. "But your mother and I will have to discuss it and pray about it. We will let you know in the morning."

"Yes, Pappa." Millie gave her father a kiss, and then gave one to Mamma and Aunt Wealthy before she went to bed. She could hear their voices in earnest conversation as she climbed the stairs, but she tried hard not to listen.

When Millie sat down to breakfast the next morning, she found a cowbell by her plate.

"What's this, Pappa?" she asked.

"Why, I thought you might like it. You will need something to call your scholars to class."

"Really?" she jumped from her chair and gave him a hug.

Before a week had passed, Millie had established a routine. Her daily teaching job began with a time of private prayer and Scripture reading in a corner of her room. After breakfast, she gathered her students in the sitting room for prayer. Reading, penmanship, and sums were finished by noon, with Millie grading papers as her scholars worked.

Marcia or Aunt Wealthy often looked in with a kiss and an encouraging word, and sometimes sat to help with corrections. Ru, who was more advanced in his studies, worked alone in his room and recited his lessons for Pappa, when they met for the noon meal. After they were done, and the little ones were released to play, Ru worked in the yard, or went to Pappa's office, or met his friends. Bill Chetwood, York Monocker, and Wallace Ormsby had incorporated Ru into their circle, though at eleven he was the youngest of the group.

Millie's Unsettled Season

Millie was also becoming friends with more of the girls in Pleasant Plains, even Helen Monocker, who rarely agreed with Millie but never seemed to remember their disagreements for very long.

Millie's favorite time of the day was when she could walk to Keiths' hill to read her Bible or just to talk to Jesus. She found that she had much more patience with her students if she prayed for them, spending time talking to Jesus about their needs. At the swing one day, Millie realized that she hadn't even thought of pinching Cyril or Don in the longest time. It was strange, she couldn't remember when the impulse had stopped troubling her. Mamma's prayer had worked — Jesus was making her more patient! And the strangest thing was how it had happened. She hadn't tried to stop pinching at all. She had just tried to be like Jesus. He was changing her heart a little bit at a time. Millie made the swing fly that day, almost touching heaven with her toes.

CHAPTER

17

Answered
Prayers

*The entire law is summed up
in a single command:
"Love your neighbor
as yourself."*

GALATIANS 5:14

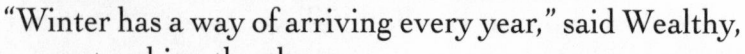

h, do you think it's come at last?" Lu was clearly focusing on the tiny snowflakes falling outside the window, rather than the Bible lesson this Sabbath morning. Even inside the church, the morning air was cold enough to make clouds when they breathed, but the ground outside was still brown and bare.

"Winter has a way of arriving every year," said Wealthy, who was teaching the class.

"Oh, but Miss Stanhope, you don't understand," Helen explained. "It's not winter we want, it's snow!" She threw her arms wide and spun around. "White, beautiful snow."

"Enough for a sleigh ride," Lu said, as if that explained everything.

"It's the Christmas social," Millie said, a little annoyed with herself for being as excited as Helen and Lu. Her friends had been talking about nothing but the social for weeks, the splendid dinner, formal dance, carolling, and sleigh ride. Bill Chetwood had been describing the delights of the huge potluck to Ru. The girls talked of almost nothing but new dresses and dancing, and Millie couldn't wait to wear her new, grown-up gown.

"The social," Aunt Wealthy said, setting her Bible down. "I see," she said with a twinkle in her eye. "And is the Christmas social more important than Joshua and the battle of Jericho?"

The young people looked at her a bit dismayed.

"It's just..." Bill began.

"The Bible all happened so long ago," Helen finished. The rest of the class looked relieved that someone had said it, and it hadn't been them.

Millie waited. She had seen that twinkle in Aunt Wealthy's eye before.

"It did happen long ago," Aunt Wealthy agreed. "But it happened to people just like you. Did you ever think of that? And most of the stories that were written down were the big, important battles. But don't you think God cared about Joshua on the days when he wasn't marching around Jericho?"

"Well, I suppose He did," Bill ventured. "Doesn't the Bible say God loves us?"

" 'For God so loved the world that He gave His one and only Son,' " Wealthy quoted. "And if you love someone, do you care what happens to them only on certain days?"

"No," said Celestia Ann. "You care every day, and night, too. Jes' like it says in Psalm 23, 'The Lord is my shepherd'… He is always watching out for you!"

"I'll tell you a secret," Wealthy said, lowering her voice. "God cares about the Christmas social. He cares about fun."

Helen looked at her doubtfully. "Damaris Drybread says that we should be solemn all of the time. I know she won't dance a step at the social. And she knows her Bible. She was our Bible teacher before you came."

"Hmmmmph," Wealthy said. "Do you know what I am going to do when I get to heaven?"

The class shook their heads.

"I'm going to a wedding feast. See—it says so right here." She flipped her Bible open to Revelations 19:6 and read, " 'Then I heard what sounded like a great multitude, like the roar of rushing waters and like loud peals of thunder, shouting: "Hallelujah! For our Lord God Almighty reigns. Let us rejoice and be glad and give him glory! For the wedding of the Lamb has come." ' " Have you ever been to a wedding?"

"When my sister Annabelle married Joel Husker, we had us a feast," Celestia Ann said. "And a fiddler, too, and folks danced all night!"

"That's right!" Wealthy said. "A wedding feast is a party, like a social. And Jesus Himself is going to be there! Now why were you worried about snow?"

"We always have a sleigh ride," Lu explained. "And sing carols. But we usually have plenty of snow by now. And there haven't been but a few flakes this year."

"Well," said Wealthy, folding her hands. "Let's just talk to Him about that." By the time class was over, they had talked to the Lord about snow, dresses, and shoes. Bill had put in a special request for someone to be inspired to bring a rhubarb pie. Everyone was laughing, and it was almost as much fun as the social itself.

Millie walked home with Claudina that afternoon, Lu and Helen by their side. Even though it was a month until Christmas, the Chetwoods' house was bright with holiday decorations. Wreaths of evergreen made bright with holly berries filled the whole house with a delicious Christmas smell. The Chetwoods were always the first family to decorate for the season, Claudina explained. Once Mrs. Chetwood hung the greens, the whole town began to break out in holiday cheer. She served the girls hot cider and ham sandwiches to eat.

"Have you started your gown?" Claudina asked.

"It's almost done," Millie said. "I'm just sewing on the French lace."

"Emerald green silk and French lace?" Claudina said. "Why, Millie Keith, with your angel eyes and golden hair, you will be the belle of the ball!"

"I'm sure that is not true," Millie said. "Besides, I have a dreadful feeling I will catch cold, and my nose will be bright red!"

"Oh, me too!" Claudina said. "I am so nervous. I know I am going to trip on my gown. Or spill punch on the sleeve of a stranger."

"A handsome stranger," giggled Lu.

Finally, the young ladies took their leave. Bill and Claudina offered to walk them home, as it was growing dark, and still talking about the details of the party, the girls accepted. They dropped Lu at her home first, then turned up the bluff toward the Big Yellow House. The sun had not yet set, but heavy gray clouds darkened the sky.

"I believe Someone was listening as Aunty prayed," Millie said as a harsh gust of cold wind nearly knocked her over.

"Let it snow!" Bill yelled, raising his arms to the sky. The wind seemed to answer, pushing them along.

"Brrrrrr. It's getting cold," Claudina said.

"You have only a thin jacket," Millie said. "I can almost see my house from here. Run home, and I'll see you on Sunday!"

They said their good-byes and Millie hurried toward home. As she neared the blacksmith's shop, she saw two figures coming up the street, huddled together. The taller one seemed to be protecting the smaller one, sheltering her from the wind.

"It's Rhoda Jane," Millie said to herself as they drew closer. "And little Min. It looks like they forgot their coats, too. Good thing they're almost home."

"Hi, Rhoda Jane!" Millie began as she caught up with them, but the look on Rhoda Jane's face took her breath

away. There was something fierce in Rhoda Jane's eyes. She opened her mouth to say something, but suddenly gripped Min's shoulder instead. She swayed for a moment, and collapsed.

"Rhoda Jane!" Min cried, squatting beside her. "Get up!"

"What's wrong?" Millie cried, kneeling beside the fallen girl.

"I told her to eat her potato," Min said. "But she said I could eat it. I was so hungry! I'm sorry, Rhoda Jane. Please get up!"

Millie suddenly felt as if something large and dark had walked by, touching them with its shadow. There was something here, something terrible, that she did not understand yet, but she knew she had to act quickly. "Lord," she prayed aloud. "Help us!" She stripped off her coat and wrapped it around the girl laying on the ground.

"Run and get your mother, Min," she said. "Run!"

"Ma's gone to work," Min whimpered. "Only Gordon's home."

"Get Gordon, then!" Millie said.

The little girl ran for home, and Millie cradled Rhoda Jane's head in her lap, trying to block the wind as huge, fat snowflakes started falling.

It seemed like an eternity before Gordon came running through the darkness.

"Rhoda Jane?" he called, kneeling beside her and shaking her shoulder. She groaned. "She's going to be all right. Soon as we get some food in her. She's got weak blood, that's all," his voice sounded choked, "That's all."

"I do not have weak blood," Rhoda Jane said. "I just got dizzy."

Millie's Unsettled Season

Millie had never been so relieved to hear anyone's voice.

"Let's keep the coat on her while you take her home," Millie said.

"I do not need a coat!" Rhoda Jane said.

"Hush," Gordon said, scooping her up in his arms.

Millie followed along behind Gordon as he carried his sister, and held the door open for him when he reached the smithy. It was bitterly cold and almost completely dark inside.

"Where are the matches and lamp?" Millie asked. Gordon nodded in the direction of a wooden box on a nearby table. Fumbling in the dark, Millie found a stone and the matches. She struck the match, found the lamp, lit it quickly, and the room began to come to light—bare wooden walls with knots missing where the wind could come in, and a bare wooden floor. The only furnishings were two chairs, a table, and a small wood stove. A shelf of books against the back wall was the only thing in the room that spoke of anything but poverty. She remembered how embarrassed she had felt when Claudina and Lu had come to the Big Yellow House to welcome her to town, and her heart suddenly ached for Rhoda Jane.

"Run and get some blankets, Minerva," Gordon said. "I want to put Sister in here until she is warm." He settled Rhoda Jane in a chair by the wood stove and set to work building a fire. The little girl ran into the next room and came back with a thin blanket, and Gordon tucked it around his sister. "I told you to eat your own potato," he said. "Now look what's happened!"

"Hush," Rhoda Jane said, glancing at Millie. "I'm fine. Can we offer you some tea?"

Millie wanted to say no and run from this place, but she couldn't. "Yes," she said, as if it were the Chetwoods' sitting room. "I would love a cup of tea."

Gordon put a kettle on the wood stove, and Millie edged closer to the warmth as it started to steam. He dropped the leaves in the teapot, poured the hot water over them, and set them to steep while he peeled three potatoes. He set a skillet on the stovetop to heat while he poured the tea.

"Would you like some sugar?" Rhoda Jane asked.

"We can't have sugar," Min said. "It's only for company or Christmas!"

"Hush, now," Gordon said, putting a scant spoonful in Millie's cup. "One spoon or two?" he asked.

"Two," Millie said, sure that he would be insulted if she turned down the sweet, or even if she asked for just one. *Lord, forgive me!* Millie prayed as Gordon put two heaping spoonfuls in Millie's tea, and then the same in Rhoda Jane's.

"Gord…" Rhoda Jane began, but he interrupted her. "Drink it," he said. "I'll put the potatoes on."

Millie drank her weak, too sweet tea, thinking of the buckets of milk and cream in the shed at the Big Yellow House. How could she ever have felt poor? Her eyes went back to the books.

"You like to read?" Rhoda Jane asked, surprised. "I thought you were like Claudina, with a head full of fluff."

"I love reading," Millie said, flushing a little for her friend's sake. "My Aunt Wealthy has the most wonderful library back home. I think I miss it almost as much as I miss my friends!"

"Father used to read to us every night," Rhoda Jane said. "I miss his voice."

"Rhoda Jane reads to us now," Min said. "She says you don't need friends if you have books."

Books never judge you because of your clothes. They don't mind if you don't have money. And…and they will still sit with you, even

if your house is cold. Millie had not felt more kindness or hospitality in any home in Pleasant Plains. When the others offered her tea, she knew they had plenty for themselves. The Lightcaps were giving her their best, all they had. *I will give you the treasures of darkness, riches stored in secret places...* Millie drew in her breath as she remembered. *Could the Lightcaps be the riches God promised? They certainly are hidden in darkness!*

The front door opened with a sharp gust of wind, and Mrs. Lightcap and Emmaretta blew in. "Good heavens!" she said, dropping her heavy load of laundry and stooping to unwrap Emmaretta, who looked like a mummy bundled in a blanket. "I didn't realize we had company!"

"Rhoda Jane wasn't feeling well," Millie said. "Would you like me to send for Dr. Chetwood?"

"No," Mrs. Lightcap said quickly. "I think we will be fine. Won't you stay for supper?"

Millie tried hard not to look at the one skillet of potatoes.

"No, thank you," she said politely. "My mother is probably worried about me already."

"It's dark out," Mrs. Lightcap said. "And the wind would take a candle. How about you carry the lamp for her, Gordon?"

Gordon carried their only lamp, leaving his family waiting in the dark until he returned, and he and Millie hurried up the hill toward the bright lights of her home. She left her coat, and he hadn't any, so they walked quickly with their shoulders hunched against the wind. When she reached the step, Millie turned.

"Thank you for the tea," she said. "It was delicious."

Gordon Lightcap had a beautiful smile.

CHAPTER

18

Broken Hearts

He who despises his neighbor sins, but blessed is he who is kind to the needy.

PROVERBS 14:21

"*M*illie!" Stuart said when she came in the door. "I was just setting out to look for you! The snow is starting to pile up. I think it is safe to say there will be sleigh rides this winter!"

"Oh, Pappa, I don't care about sleigh rides at all!" Millie poured out her story of the Lightcap home.

"I thought you knew the Lightcaps was poor," Celestia Ann said. "They kinda wandered into Pleasant Plains on accident two years ago. But their Pap got sick, and when he died, they just stuck. Gordy shoes horses and can put a rim on a wheel, using the tools that used to be his pa's. Mrs. Lightcap takes in wash."

The Keiths were subdued as they sat down to supper. As soon as the younger ones had all been tucked in their warm beds, Millie went to the parlor with Pappa and Mamma and Aunt Wealthy. Celestia Ann brought in a tray of tea, and Stuart invited her to stay.

"I don't understand, Pappa," Millie said. "If God cares about little things, doesn't He care about the Lightcaps?"

"Of course He does," Stuart said. "Sometimes He uses His children here on earth to reach out to people. Perhaps He can use your hands, Millie, to help them."

"Mine?" Millie was embarrassed to realize that she had never reached out to Rhoda Jane. "But how? Should we go over there tonight with money and food?"

"You'd shame 'em to death if you took them a thing," Celestia Ann said. "All that fam'ly has left is guts and pride. And if you go givin' 'em charity, you take that away, too."

"I think she's right," Aunt Wealthy said. "But what can we do?"

"I'm sure I can send some work Gordon's way, if I speak a few words to my clients," Stuart said.

"Emmaretta's big enough to milk a cow," Celestia Ann suggested. "An' churn butter too. And Belle's always givin' more than we need. I could ask her if she wants a job milkin' and churnin' and tell her to keep the extry."

"Good idea," Stuart said.

"But I want to do more," Millie said. Her mother kissed her on the forehead.

"You've already begun, Millie mine. Tonight you allowed them into your heart. And your broken, compassionate heart is a prayer rising up to heaven."

Marcia wrapped her in a hug. "We will all watch and pray. I know the Lord uses people who are willing, and I for one am willing to do anything at all to help our neighbors."

That night as Millie lay in her bed, her heart was broken, and the only way to ease the pain was to lift it up to her Heavenly Father. *Rhoda Jane doesn't have much food, Lord. And maybe she wouldn't take it if it were offered. And she doesn't have any friends…show me what to do!* Pictures of the cold, bare room ran through her mind, but she always came back to the shelf of books.

When Millie woke the next morning, the snow had covered the earth in a soft, white blanket, and the frost had left lace on the windowpanes. She dressed quickly and spent a quiet half hour with her Bible before she went downstairs.

"Do you mind if I visit Rhoda Jane this morning, Mamma?" Millie asked. "I want to see how she is."

"Of course you may." Her mother smiled.

Millie took her copy of *Ivanhoe*, tucked it under her arm, wrapped up in her warmest cloak, and started down the hill. The air cut like a knife, but the ice crystals made rainbows, a million tiny promises, caught in every tree. Millie stopped for a quick prayer before she reached the Lightcaps' door.

"Give me courage, Lord," she said, then lifted her hand and knocked.

Rhoda Jane answered the door, looking a little pale. "Why, Millie! I wasn't expecting you so soon! The coat's in the other room. Just let me get it…"

"Thank you," Millie said. "But I didn't come for the coat. I was wondering if you might let me borrow a book."

"Borrow a book?" Rhoda Jane looked blank.

"I couldn't help but notice your library," Millie said. "And I have been so starved for good books. I finished this one," she held out her precious copy of *Ivanhoe*, "and I thought…perhaps we might trade. Only for a little while."

Rhoda Jane reached out slowly and took the book, but her eyes were searching Millie's face.

"That's all you want, to borrow one of my books?"

"Yes," Millie said. "I mean no! I do want something more, Rhoda Jane. I want someone to talk to. I haven't had anyone to talk to…I mean, really talk to…in months."

"Come in," Rhoda Jane said.

Millie stomped the powdered snow off her boots and followed Rhoda Jane into the kitchen. The stove was warm, and the kitchen smelled of fried potatoes. Emmaretta and Minerva sat at the table, with a book open before them. There was a piece of slate with chalk letters on the table.

"You're teaching them yourself!" Millie exclaimed.

"We don't have enough money to send them to school," Rhoda Jane said. "And I wouldn't send them to Miss Drybones even if we did."

"I wouldn't either," Millie said. "I'm teaching Zillah and Adah, too." She explained briefly about Cyril and Don's raid on the schoolhouse.

Rhoda Jane smiled. "I heard about that," she said. "Help yourself to a book."

Millie took her time examining the books on the shelf, and finally chose a book of poetry by William Blake.

"Thank you," she managed, and ran out of things to say.

"You are welcome," said Rhoda Jane as she led her to the door. "Stop by when you have finished it. That's one of my favorites."

Millie split her time between devouring poems, working on her green gown, and dreaming about the social. Stuart had found some people with work for Gordon, and the ring of the hammer on the anvil in the distance made her smile. When she had finished the book of poetry, she took it and her copy of *The Last of the Mohicans* and walked down the hill again.

"Hello, Millie," Rhoda Jane said, opening the door. "Won't you come in? The girls are playing house right now, so we can talk." She offered Millie a seat, and heated water for tea, which she served with cream and biscuits.

"How did you like the book?" Rhoda Jane asked when she placed a steaming cup in front of Millie.

"I loved it." Millie smiled, and quoted:

Tyger! Tyger! burning bright
In the forests of the night,
What immortal hand or eye
Could frame thy fearful symmetry?

Rhoda Jane nodded and joined her for the second verse:

In what distant deeps or skies
Burnt the fire of thine eyes?
On what wings dare he aspire?
What the hand dare seize the fire?

They finished the poem together, while Emmaretta looked on, open-mouthed.

"Blake's words are like thunder!" Millie said. "What about you? Did you enjoy *Ivanhoe*?"

"I fear I am in love with him, and woe is me." Rhoda Jane put her hand to her forehead, her wrist limp. "Woe is me, for he loves fair Rowena well!"

This time, both girls laughed. "I do have a question, though." She pulled the book from the shelf and opened the cover to Millie's bookplate.

"This book belongs to Jesus?"

Millie looked down at her own writing. It seemed so long ago now, a hundred years at least. Millie began with the story of the book, but as it spilled out, she found that it was all mixed up with how hard it had been to leave her friends in Lansdale. She was surprised to realize that she hadn't told anyone the story of her trip since she arrived.

As Millie described Aunt Wealthy's saving Dr. Percival Fox, Rhoda Jane was laughing so hard that tears ran down

her face. But when she described Dr. Fox's decision to live for Jesus, Rhoda Jane grew solemn again.

"I'm sure that it is very comforting for you, Millie," she said. "I almost wish I had faith in something like that."

"Why, Rhoda Jane, do you mean you don't believe in God? Surely you can't read the Bible without knowing, just knowing that He loves you!"

"That is one book I have never read," Rhoda Jane said. "When my father was sick, Drybones brought me a Bible. She said that my father would not be sick if we were not sinners, and that perhaps if we read the Bible we would mend our ways, and he would get well. My father died that night," Rhoda Jane said matter of factly. "If anyone else had given me that book, even Reverend Lord, I might have read it. But it was Damaris Drybread. I burned it."

Millie was horrified, and her heart was breaking all at once. How could anyone, anyone burn God's Word? But how could someone say something so horrible? What if her own dear Pappa lay dying?

"It's not like that, Rhoda Jane," Millie said. "I'm sure God didn't kill your father to punish you! It must have broken His heart…"

"I don't want to talk about it, really," Rhoda Jane said. "Do you want to borrow another book?"

"Yes," Millie said, bringing out her copy of *The Last of the Mohicans*. "And I have another for you."

Millie selected Shakespeare's *Much Ado about Nothing*, said her good-byes and hurried up the hill.

Cyril and Don had built a snow fort in front of the Big Yellow House.

"Who goes there," Cyril bellowed as Millie approached.

"Be ye friend or foe?" Don asked.

"I be your sister," Millie said. "And I want to get inside."

"No," said Don lobbing a snowball at her. "No one passes!"

Millie ducked her head and charged through the hail of snowballs to the front door. She slammed it behind her, and was taking off her cloak when someone knocked. She opened the door to find Claudina and Helen standing on the step. Claudina held a package in her arms. There were no snowball marks on her cloak or the paper of her package, and she had a beautiful smile on her face.

"How did you get past the fort?" Millie asked.

"Simple," Claudina said. "I told them I would kiss them once for each snowball they threw. They didn't throw even one! Millie, my gown has arrived. And the slippers. I just had to show you! But you were just coming in! Where have you been? I haven't seen you for ages!"

"I was visiting with Rhoda Jane," Millie said.

A look of dismay came over Helen's face. "Millie, you must be careful. Everyone knows that this," she motioned to the make-do furnishings around her, "is temporary and that the Keiths will be building a fine new home. But Mrs. Lightcap…Why, she does our laundry, Millie. Charity is one thing, but friendship is quite another."

Millie was trying to think of a reply, but Claudina continued as if there had been no interruption.

"Look at this." She pulled a pale blue velvet gown from the bag. "Made in Chicago by my mother's seamstress," she said, holding it up and waltzing around the room. "Isn't it beautiful! And Mother says I may wear my hair up with silk roses. What do you think?"

"I think you will be beautiful," Millie said. "And quite grown up."

"Now you must let us see your gown," Helen said.

"Oh, no." Millie didn't feel like talking to them at all. "I don't want anyone to see it until it's finished."

The girls stayed and chatted for an hour, though Millie's mind was clearly elsewhere.

"Isn't that your father coming home?" Claudina asked at last. "I didn't realize it was so late. It's time to be going, Helen."

Millie was glad to see them to the door, but gladder still to see her own dear Pappa coming up the hill. They passed the fort unmolested under his watchful eye, then turned and waved to Millie before they started home.

Millie could scarcely keep her mind on her sewing that night, as she told her parents about her day, and what Damaris Drybread had done when Mr. Lightcap lay dying.

"Ouch," she said, laying her seamwork aside and sucking a bead of blood from the finger her needle had pierced. "How could anyone be so horrible?"

"Damaris Drybones," Stuart said, "might be a fitting name after all."

"Now, Stuart," said Marcia. "You know that Jesus loves her."

"That's true, my dear," he said. "And I ask your pardon and His forgiveness. But I do think she has done a great deal of harm where she should have done good."

CHAPTER

19

Christmas Wonders

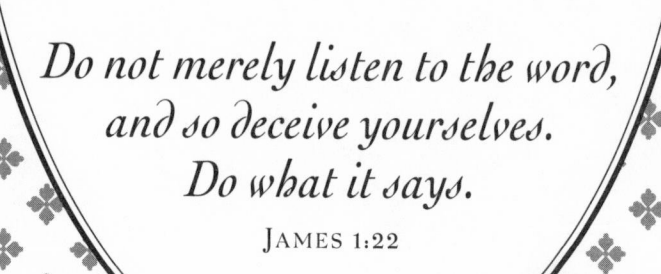

*Do not merely listen to the word,
and so deceive yourselves.
Do what it says.*

JAMES 1:22

*M*illie found teaching more and more difficult as her students' attention turned to the excitement of the season. The Lord had answered Aunt Wealthy's prayers with an abundance of snow. Rupert and his friends built a sledding hill, packing the snow into heaps and piles to make their sleds leap. Gordon joined them when work allowed.

"You should see his sled fly!" Rupert reported. "He made the runners himself, and no one is faster!"

Since the snow was too deep to climb to her swing, Millie sometimes joined Ru in his sledding after lessons, but more often than not she would walk down the hill to the Lightcaps. She understood now why Aunt Wealthy liked to walk as she prayed. For every trip to the neighboring house, Millie prayed the whole way, asking God to help her show her new friend His love.

Rhoda Jane normally kept her students seated at the table well past their noon meal. Three days before the social, Millie arrived just as Min finished wiping soup from her slate.

"I spilt my soup on it," she explained matter of factly. "Because I was writing down the in. . . in. . . ."

"Ingredients," Rhoda Jane said.

"Yeah," Min said. "That's what's in here!"

"You run your schoolroom so efficiently," Millie giggled. "Really Rhoda Jane, Em and Min are reading very well. And I am sure you are better at teaching sums than I am. Wait a minute!" Millie sank into a chair. "I have just had the most wonderful idea!"

"If it is anything like your last idea, I think you should forget about it right now, before any damage is done," Rhoda Jane said.

"Teaching subtraction and addition using gumdrops would have worked very well if Cyril hadn't eaten them all, and you know it," Millie said, smiling.

"At least he understood the subtraction part," Rhoda Jane laughed.

"It was a good idea," Millie insisted. "But this one's better. What if we put our school rooms together tomorrow? It will be too hard to concentrate on anything with just one day left before the social. We could make it a party. I could teach reading, and you could teach sums. I'm sure the girls would love it. We could meet in my sitting room, where there are more chairs…"

"Please, Rhoda Jane!" Min said, clapping her hands. "It would be a real school!"

Marcia and Aunt Wealthy quickly approved the plan, and the next morning attendance in Millie's school had doubled. Emmaretta and Minerva brought their own meals of cornbread and boiled eggs in pails, and Zillah and Adah insisted on having their food in pails, too. Snowflakes were falling once again, so Millie spread a tablecloth on the floor and they had a picnic while Rhoda Jane read aloud.

After the picnic, Zillah invited Emmaretta and Minerva to participate in a Christmas play; they would have costumes and lines to memorize. The boys would join them.

"You can be an angel," Zillah told Cyril. "And Don will be a shepherd."

"Wahooo!" Don said, twirling his rope like a sling. "Wannago's gonna be the sheep!"

Cyril scratched his head and considered. "I don't wanna be a Christmas angel," he said. "I like the smiting kind, the ones that marched in the treetops when David went to war, or the ones with chariots and horses on the hills around the town where Elijah and his servant stayed. Now those are angels!"

"They were the same angels," Millie said.

"Are you sure they were the very same ones? Christmas angels seem kind of like sissies. All they did was sing," said Cyril suspiciously.

"God has lots of angels, so they might not have been exactly the same ones. But they were singing praises to God," Millie said, "just like we do in church, or in the evening when Pappa leads us. Does Pappa sound like a sissy?"

"No," Cyril had to admit. "He sounds happy."

"Do you think that the shepherds were sissies?"

"No!" Don yelled. "Shepherds had to stay out all night alone, fighting wolves and bears and robbers!" He punched an imaginary robber. "Pow!"

"I want to be a shepherd," Fan said.

"You can't." Don patted her head. "You're a girl. Girls can't fight wolves and bears."

"Can too!" Fan yelled.

"Can not!" Don yelled back.

"What is all of this yelling about?" Aunt Wealthy asked, coming into the room.

"Don says I can't be a shepherd," the little girl said, throwing herself against Aunt Wealthy in despair.

"Well, that is true," Aunt Wealthy said. "You cannot be a shepherd. You will have to be a shepherdess. You will have to be strong and brave and beautiful. Like Rachel. She was

a shepherdess, so she had to be brave. And she was so beautiful that Jacob was willing to work for seven years so she would be his bride."

"He said girls can't fight wolves and bears," Fan said, still not certain.

"Of course they can't," Aunt Wealthy agreed. "Not by themselves. But neither can boys. Do you think David fought lions and bears all by himself?"

"No," Ru said. "David said the Lord delivered him from the paw of the lion and the bear."

"It's God's job to help us fight the lions and bears," Aunt Wealthy said. "Whether we are boys or girls, it's our job to trust Him."

"I still think the Christmas angels were sissies," said Cyril, folding his arms.

"If the shepherds were brave, then the angels were not sissies." Millie opened her Bible to Luke 2:9. " 'An angel of the Lord appeared to them, and the glory of the Lord shown around them, and they were terrified.' "

"You mean they hafta be terrified of me?" Cyril asked. "Well, that ain't too bad!"

The dispute over angels and shepherds resolved, the children ran to Zillah's room to work on their parts and costumes.

"The Keiths are definitely the most peculiar people I have ever met," Rhoda Jane said, as Aunt Wealthy ushered the last of the little ones out of the room. "All of that is in this book?" she asked as she flipped through the pages of Millie's Bible.

"Oh, yes," Millie said, "and lots more." She wanted so desperately to tell Rhoda Jane about Jesus, and how He had died for the world. That was the real reason for Christmas. She said a quick prayer and waited for the right words to come to her.

Celestia Ann arrived instead.

"Lookit who blew in," she said, ushering Helen, Lu, and Claudina into the room, and helping them out of their coats.

Millie's heart sank, but she greeted her visitors cordially. The afternoon was immediately focused on the Christmas social, Helen and Lu giggling over who would ask them to dance, their hairstyles and what, if any, jewelry their mothers would allow them to wear.

"Oh," Claudina said, suddenly seeming to realize that Rhoda Jane was not joining the chatter, "are you going to the social, Rhoda Jane?"

Rhoda Jane flushed, as all eyes turned to her.

"And is Gordon going?" Now all eyes shifted to Claudina, who turned pink in turn. Helen's eyebrows went up just a hair.

"Gordon plans to attend," Rhoda Jane said. "He loves to dance."

Claudina turned even pinker, and Lu giggled.

"I did not know that any of the Lightcaps danced," Helen said. "I have never seen either of you at a social before."

"Perhaps our social circles have simply not collided until now," Rhoda Jane said dryly.

"Then I will be pleasantly surprised, I'm sure," Helen said. "After all, everyone is invited," she said, glancing at Millie.

"I'm sure we will enjoy the company," Rhoda Jane replied.

"Would anyone like some hot cider?" Millie asked, desperate to change the subject.

"I would," Claudina said quickly.

"I'll help you prepare it," Rhoda Jane said, standing up. She followed Millie into the kitchen. Once there, Rhoda Jane gripped the edge of the table and leaned against it.

"I shouldn't have said that," she said. "I can't go. But Gordon is going, and he does love to dance."

"Why can't you?" Millie asked, pulling out a chair for her friend.

Rhoda Jane just laughed. "Shall I wear this?" She smoothed her faded calico. "Or my other dancing gown?"

"Oh. Oh." Millie said, sitting down beside her. How could she not have thought of it? Of course, Rhoda Jane had no dress to wear. And with one day until the social, there was no time to sew one, even if she had fabric.

"In Lansdale I traded gowns with my friends all of the time," Millie said. "We are about the same size. You could borrow one of mine. I know we could make it work."

"I couldn't do that."

"Why not?" Millie said. "I would. I wore a borrowed gown to a dance last year. Besides, you said you were going! Don't you want to see Helen's face when you and Gordon arrive?"

"You really think we can make one of your gowns work?"

"I know we can," said Millie. "You just come over a few hours before the social tomorrow. Promise?"

"I will," Rhoda Jane said and lifted her chin.

"Good," Millie squeezed her hand. "Now, let's get that cider."

After the girls had left, Millie climbed the stairs to her bedroom and opened her trunk. She pulled the yellow gown from the bottom and smoothed it on her bed. The puffed sleeves and sash with a bow were hopelessly out of style, and it did look

childish. She fingered the ink stain that Zillah had left on the hem when she borrowed it to play dress-up. Then she hung it on the wall next to her new green gown.

Marcia asked Millie to join them in the parlor for tea as Stuart put the children to bed. Millie was glad to have a moment to speak to her parents. She dropped down on the sofa with a sigh.

"You seem pensive tonight," Marcia said, putting an arm around her. "I thought you would be excited about the social and the sleigh ride."

Millie told her about the day, starting with the shared lessons, and the interruption just as Millie was prepared to talk to Rhoda Jane about God's Word, and finishing with her plan to loan Rhoda Jane a dress.

"What do you think, Mamma?" Millie asked.

When she had finished, Marcia stroked her hair. "I am so proud of you," she said. "Will you let me say a short prayer?"

Millie nodded and laid her head on her mother's shoulder.

"Please give Millie courage and wisdom and strength," Marcia prayed. "And give her Your special joy. Lord, I pray for Rhoda Jane to learn of Your love and care. Let her see how much You love her. Shine Your light through my precious Millie. In Jesus' name. Amen."

Lessons were cancelled the next morning as Millie, Aunt Wealthy, and Marcia attacked the yellow gown with scissors and needles and thread. The bow was removed, the puff on the sleeves tucked and sewed. By raising the hem

just a hair, they were almost able to hide the ink stain. It was finished by noon, and Millie stood back to look at their work.

"Well," she said, "it's not horrible."

"It's not horrible at all," said Marcia, gathering Millie in her arms. "It will be lovely."

Rhoda Jane arrived at three, still uncertain.

"I don't see how a gown of yours will fit me," she said. "I'm two inches taller!"

"Well, let's try it and see." Millie led the way up the stairs to her room. Rhoda Jane looked at the two dresses hanging side by side in Millie's room. It was clear from the stain on the hem which one was used. Rhoda Jane took the yellow dress off its hanger and held it up in front of her. "It is pretty," she said.

Millie swallowed hard. She wasn't sure until this moment that she could get through this without tears, but suddenly she knew she could.

"Oh, that's not your gown," she said. "The green one is for you. The yellow one would be too short, don't you think?"

Rhoda Jane sucked in her breath. "The green one? Millie, are you sure?"

"Of course, I'm sure," Millie said. "It's too long for me, and we don't have time to hem it now." It wasn't lying not to mention that she had planned to wear heels. "So you will have to wear that one."

Aunt Wealthy helped Rhoda Jane with her gown and hair, while Marcia helped Millie. Celestia Ann insisted on doing everything herself, and her wild curls and mischievous grin were just the same when she came upstairs to show off her gown and the shawl Wealthy had loaned her.

"How are you gettin' on? You look mighty nice, Millie."

Millie spun in front of the mirror and sighed. They had done wonders for the yellow dress, but the style was still too young, and if her dancing slippers had had the least hint of a heel, the skirt would have been too short. Her hair did shine like a river of gold where it fell over her shoulders though.

Celestia Ann gasped as Wealthy led Rhoda Jane into the room.

"It's Rebecca!" Zillah declared, clapping her hands. "Just like in *Ivanhoe*, Millie!"

"You're so pretty!" Adah cried.

Wealthy had swept the girl's hair up and fastened it with combs. Her brown eyes were huge in her heart-shaped face.

Wealthy turned Rhoda Jane toward the mirror, and in that instant, when Rhoda Jane caught sight of her reflection, Millie was sure she had done the right thing. Rhoda Jane's mouth opened, then shut again, as she touched the French lace at her throat. She shook her head, and burst out in tears.

"No, no, no!" Wealthy said, producing a handkerchief. "No crying! You don't want your eyes all red for the party! No crying!"

"Of course not," Rhoda Jane said between sobs, crying even harder.

Wealthy had managed to dry the tears by the time Rhoda Jane left to help Gordon get ready.

"We'll meet you there, Millie," she said, giving her a hug.

Millie finished her own preparations, and stood with Celestia Ann, Ru, and Stuart and Marcia, as Aunt Wealthy inspected them.

"Oh, you all look so beautiful!" she said. "I am sure you will have the time of my life!"

"We will try," Stuart said seriously.

"And don't you worry about the little ones. Wannago and I are perfectly capable of caring for the lot."

"Of course you are," said Marcia.

"We really should be going," Stuart said, looking at his pocketwatch.

"Aren't you forgetting something?" Marcia asked.

"I don't think so," Stuart said.

"Stuart!"

"Oh, you must mean this!" He pulled a slender velvet box out of his pocket.

"Miss Mildred Keith, you will no doubt be the loveliest girl at the social tonight. And I humbly ask you to hold one dance for me. But until then, I want you to have a token of my great esteem for you. Will you do me the honor of accepting this little gift?" Stuart opened the box for Millie to see inside. Resting on the black velvet was a golden chain with a single pearl.

Millie was speechless as her father laid the necklace around her throat and her mother checked the clasp to be sure it was secure.

"This is a Christmas and early birthday present," her mother said, kissing her forehead.

Millie was absolutely glowing as she picked up her cloak and muff, and kissed Aunt Wealthy good night.

The Pleasant Plains Pavilion was used for everything from livestock auctions to town meetings, Sunday afternoon meals, and hymn sing-alongs after church. But one

night each year, in mid-December, the simple place was transformed. The rafters were draped with evergreen garlands, a holiday feast laid out, and tables lit with cozy lanterns and candles.

Millie heard the music growing stronger as they approached the pavilion. The lively sounds of fiddle, guitar, and piano floated on the evening air and greeted them in full force as they entered.

Everyone was dressed in their very finest, and laughter rippled from groups of people already gathered in the hall. Stuart soon joined a group of men discussing business matters and politics, and Marcia wandered over to a group of ladies giving finishing touches to the tables and offered to help.

Millie, Rupert, and their friends clustered together. The young men were smiling and joking, the young ladies looking beautiful in their much-worried-over gowns. Claudina wore her pale blue velvet gown with matching cape. Her long dark curls were held together with a mother-of-pearl comb. Lucilla and Helen's dresses were cut in very different styles but made from similar shades of deep crimson satin. All the girls admired Millie's new pearl necklace.

"A Christmas surprise from your parents? How lovely!" Lucilla said.

"Yes…lovely," Helen said, giving Millie's gown a puzzled glance, and Millie saw her eyes travel down to the hint of a stain on the hem.

Celestia Ann saw the look and smiled. "That's the rage in Paree," she said.

Millie blushed.

At that moment a handsome couple stepped in the door. Gordon Lightcap stood tall, holding the arm of his sister.

Millie's Unsettled Season

Rhoda Jane had been beautiful at Millie's house; in the soft light of the ballroom she was breathtaking.

The girls rushed to greet her. They made her turn around in dizzying circles so they could admire her lovely dress.

"Why, Rhoda Jane, that lace is just the perfect trimming for your gown!" Helen said "Where on earth did you get it?"

Millie's eyes met Rhoda Jane's, and she prayed that her friend would be spared any sort of embarrassment.

As if on cue, Mr. Grange announced that the dancing was to begin, and York Monocker stepped forward. He bowed ever so slightly and offered his hand to Rhoda Jane. "Miss Lightcap, you outshine the stars tonight. Would you do me the honor of granting me the first dance?" Rhoda Jane took his hand, and he led her to the floor. All eyes in the room were fixed on the couple as they swirled about the pavilion.

"Well!" Claudina said. "Rhoda Jane was certainly telling the truth when she said Lightcaps could dance!"

"My sister is a very truthful girl," Gordon said, bowing. "Would you care to dance with a Lightcap, Miss Chetwood?"

Claudina pinkened to the tip of her nose, but she took his hand and they stepped onto the dance floor.

"Rhoda Jane is the most beautiful girl here tonight," Millie said.

"The second most beautiful for sure," Celestia Ann said. "Somethin' in you sure does shine, Millie!"

Marcia and Stuart Keith made their way through the crowds to their daughter and son.

"Are you ready for your dance?" Stuart asked, offering his arm to Millie. She stepped onto the floor and followed her father's lead. As she twirled, she had flashes of Rupert trying valiantly to waltz with his mother.

Finally, Stuart leaned over and whispered in Millie's ear, "I must abandon you to save your mother's toes." Millie smiled and returned to her friends.

The hour grew late, the food was nearly gone, and even though she would never have admitted it, Millie was exhausted long before time for the midnight sleigh ride home.

The large omnibus sleigh drawn by four horses with jingling bells on their harnesses waited outside, under the light of a full golden moon. The sleigh was piled high with buffalo robes and blankets for keeping the cold at bay.

"I don't think I can move," Claudina said, after taking her seat. She was bundled in a cloak and scarf, cap and gloves, with a buffalo robe piled on her.

"You don't have to move," Celestia Ann said, snuggling in beside her. "Just sing."

The Reverend Lord and Miss Drybread sat in their midst keeping a sharp eye on them, just in case the moonlight got the best of anyone. The girls began to giggle and glance at the young men. Millie rolled her eyes.

The driver shook the reins, and with a jingle of bells, the sleigh was off, runners hissing almost silently over the snow. They sang Christmas carols and laughed until they were hoarse. Bill Chetwood and Ru, who had pretended not to be interested in the ride, ambushed them as the sleigh reached the center of town, pelting them with snowballs, then running after them and swinging up into the sleigh.

When every possible carol had been sung, and some twice, the sleigh began to drop people at their doorsteps. Shouts of good night and Merry Christmas were heard, and if any young man was bold enough to walk a young lady to her door, everyone cheered or hooted.

The sleigh was more than half empty when it started up the hill toward the Big Yellow House. Rhoda Jane leaned close to Millie.

"I know what you did, Millie," she whispered. "I just wanted to say…thank you." She slipped an envelope into Millie's muff.

Millie felt in her bag for the gift she had wrapped for Rhoda Jane. "Here."

"It's a book!" Rhoda Jane said, feeling through the paper. She tore the wrapping paper off.

"The Holy Bible," she read, holding it up to the bright moonlight. Her face went very still.

Millie held her breath as Rhoda Jane opened the book and read the inscription.

For my dear friend Rhoda Jane Lightcap.
From Mildred Eleanor Keith, Christmas of 1833.
My prayer for you is found in the Gospel of John,
    Chapter 3, Verse 16.

Millie waited for her to say something, anything, but Rhoda Jane did not even look at her. Her eyes lifted to the grim face of Damaris Drybread instead.

"Smithy," the driver called, and the sleigh stopped.

"Merry Christmas," Millie called, as Rhoda Jane stepped down. Suddenly, the robes and blankets rustled, and York leapt out.

"May I walk you to your door, Miss Lightcap?" The sleigh exploded with hoots and catcalls, but York just waved.

Rhoda Jane took his arm, and he walked her to the door, Gordon following a polite distance behind. They said good-

bye at the door, and Rhoda Jane and Gordon disappeared. York returned to the sleigh, and they were off. Millie retrieved the envelope Rhoda Jane had slipped in her muff, tearing it open with impatient fingers. The moonlight was more than bright enough to make out the words:

Dear Millie,

I wanted to give you something fine for Christmas, but all I have to offer is my friendship. I don't give it lightly, but you have been a true friend to me. And I will be yours forever.

Rhoda Jane Lightcap

The next stop the sleigh made was the Big Yellow House. Millie, Ru, and Celestia Ann jumped down and waved as their friends sped away. Millie stopped on the doorstep and looked back down the hill. There was a glow in the Lightcaps' window and sparks rising from the stovepipe.

Don't burn it up, Rhoda Jane. There is a Friend who will love you much more than I ever could. Please don't burn it up.

Millie turned the doorknob and stepped inside. She pulled off her hat and tossed her muff on the table before she realized that something was very, very wrong. Marcia stood beside the couch, one hand over her mouth. Stuart knelt beside it, with a little golden head cradled in his arms. Fan's face was pale, almost blue in the lamplight, and her eyes were closed.

"Oh, Lord, help us," Aunt Wealthy cried. "I only turned my back for an instant!"

What troubles are ahead, and will Millie's faith see her through?

When a Southern relative comes to visit, what family secrets will be revealed?

Find out in:

MILLIE'S COURAGEOUS DAYS

Book Two
of the
*A Life of Faith:
Millie Keith* Series

Available at your local bookstore

Do you want to live a life of faith?
Are you interested in having a stronger devotional life?
Millie's Daily Diary can help you!

MILLIE'S DAILY DIARY
A Personal Journal for Girls

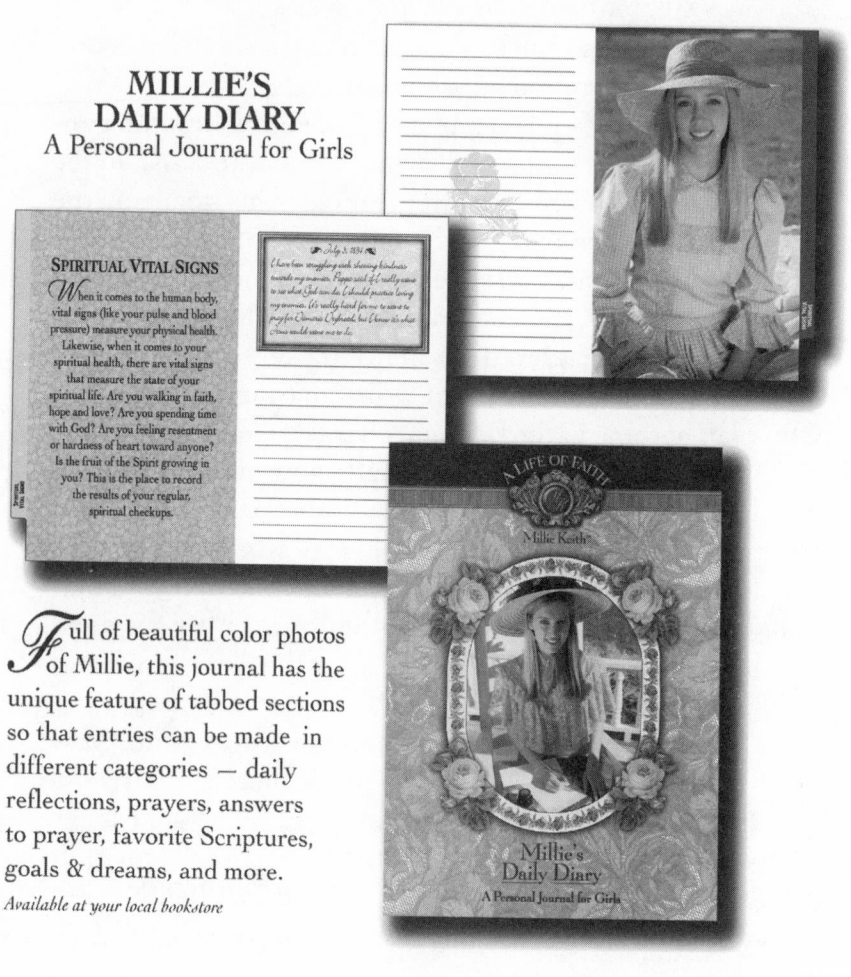

SPIRITUAL VITAL SIGNS

When it comes to the human body, vital signs (like your pulse and blood pressure) measure your physical health. Likewise, when it comes to your spiritual health, there are vital signs that measure the state of your spiritual life. Are you walking in faith, hope and love? Are you spending time with God? Are you feeling resentment or hardness of heart toward anyone? Is the fruit of the Spirit growing in you? This is the place to record the results of your regular spiritual checkups.

*F*ull of beautiful color photos of Millie, this journal has the unique feature of tabbed sections so that entries can be made in different categories — daily reflections, prayers, answers to prayer, favorite Scriptures, goals & dreams, and more.

*M*artha Finley was born on April 26, 1828, in Chillicothe, Ohio. Her mother died when Martha was quite young, and Dr. James Finley, her father, soon remarried. Martha's stepmother, Mary Finley, was a kind and caring woman who always nurtured Martha's desire to learn and supported her ambition to become a writer.

Dr. Finley was a physician and a devout Christian gentleman. He moved his family to South Bend, Indiana, in the mid-1830s in hopes of a brighter future for his family on the expanding western frontier. Growing up on the frontier as one of eight brothers and sisters surely provided the setting and likely many of the characters for Miss Finley's *Mildred Keith* novels. Considered by many to be partly autobiographical, the books present a fascinating and devoted Christian heroine in the fictional character known as Millie Keith. One can only speculate exactly how much of Martha may have been Millie and vice versa. But regardless, these books nicely complement Miss Finley's bestselling *Elsie Dinsmore* series, which was launched in 1868 and sold millions of copies. The stories of Millie Keith, Elsie's second cousin, were released eight years after the *Elsie* books as a follow-up to that series.

Martha Finley never married and never had children of her own, but she was a remarkable woman who lived a quiet life of creativity and Christian charity. She died at age 81, having written many novels, stories, and books for children and adults. Her life on earth ended in 1909, but her legacy lives on in the wonderful stories of Millie and Elsie.

Check out
www.alifeoffaith.com

- Get news about Millie and her cousin Elsie
- Find out more about the 19th century world they live in
- Learn to live a life of faith like they do
- Learn how they overcome the difficulties we all face in life
- Find out about Millie and Elsie products
- Join our girls' club

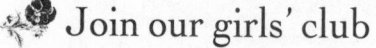

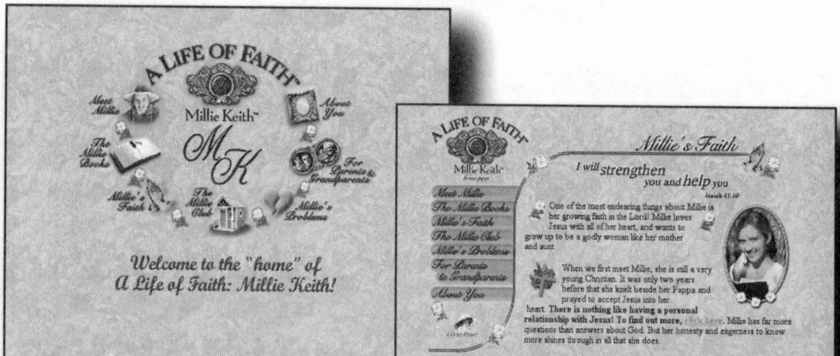

Collect all of our Elsie products!

A Life of Faith: Elsie Dinsmore Series

* Now Available as a Dramatized Audiobook!

Collect all of our Violet products!

A Life of Faith: Violet Travilla Series

MCP
Mission City Press

For more information, write to

Mission City Press at 202 Seond Ave. South,
Franklin, Tennessee 37064
or visit our Web Site at:

www.alifeoffaith.com

Beloved Literary Characters
Come to Life!

*Y*our favorite heroines, Millie Keith, Elsie Dinsmore, Violet Travilla, and Laylie Colbert are now available as lovely designer dolls from Mission City Press.

*M*ade of soft-molded vinyl, these beautiful, fully-jointed 18¾" dolls come dressed in historically-accurate clothing and accessories. They wonderfully reflect the Biblical virtues that readers have come to know and love about Millie, Elsie, Violet, and Laylie.

For more information, visit www.alifeoffaith.com or check with your local Christian retailer.

A Life of Faith® Products from Mission City Press—

"It's Like Having a Best Friend From Another Time"